ARCHETYPE

BOOK 1

I0539433

LUNCH
With

Dr. Frankenstein

by Richard R. Smith

"SUPERIOR FORM OF INTELLIGENCE"

I am always interested in feedback from my readers and would
greatly appreciate hearing from you. I would be honored if you
would post a review of this book on Amazon.com. You may
also contact me directly at my website: www.richardrsmith.com.

All illustrations and the cover design were created by WANZIE.
He can be reached at www.WanzieArcanum.com.

Acknowledgements

*The original short story was completely fabricated from my imagination. The
novel emerged from a variety of ideas and includes themes from mythology,
ancient history, religion, trans-humanism, artificial intelligence, and cultural
histories. I make no claims to know anything about these subjects and leave
true knowledge to those experts among us. My hope is this story will at least
entertain people and hopefully cause the reader to begin to question
everything they've ever learned.*

Cover design and illustrations were created by WANZIE at
Wanzie Arcanum., LLC All illustrations are © Copyrighted by
W. Christopher Wanzie and may not be reproduced or copied
without his permission.

ABOUT THE ARTIST

W. CHRISTOPHER WANZIE is an abstract graphic artist, illustrator, photographer, writer, and entrepreneur based in Los Angeles, California. He is the Owner and Creator of ARCANUM, a progressive, abstract graphic arts company creating powerful, symbolic designs that resonate across all forms of media. He contributed to the novel, "Lunch with Dr. Frankenstein," as Editor, Cover Designer, Illustrator, and Creative Consultant.

With a background in neuroscience, neuropsychology, & neurophilosophy, his work infuses scientific principles and emergent technologies with symbolic imagery inherent to spirituality and mysticism throughout human history.

His work interweaves a complexity of themes deeply rooted in the premise that all sentient beings share a common thread. The designs incorporate the sacred, resonating power of symmetry and geometry, while simultaneously fusing transhumanistic visions of the future with arcane wisdom and esoteric truths throughout all ages. His artwork emanates a visceral energy merging history, heritage, science, religion, spirituality, and mysticism into a singular vision.

Mr. Wanzie's work has been commissioned by musicians, bands, writers, businesses, and other clients to date. His new series of work titled, "THE ARCANE COLLECTIVE" will soon be released via Amazon Kindle as digital Art Books. "The Arcane Collective" will be released as multiple unique volumes for download, along with a second collection of digital art books titled, "CYBER MANDALAS" running in parallel. He is also currently writing an original screen play, and creating the concept art for the movie.

Mr. Wanzie is available for commissioned, highly-customized original artwork, and freelance assignments. He can be contacted via his official website at: www.WanzieArcanum.com , and on Facebook at Facebook.com/WChristopherWanzie. If interested in prints of the book Cover Design and/or Chapter Illustrations, please send a direct request to Mr. Wanzie's email address at WanzieArcanum@gmail.com. All illustrations can be rendered in variant colors and effects per request.

SPECIAL ACKNOWLEDGEMENTS

The Anatomical Figures utilized in ASCENSION & INVOLUNTARY CYBERNETIC RE-ANIMATION are credited to, and copyrights of, Sebastian Kaulitzki.

ABOUT THE COVER DESIGN

The book cover design, titled "THE HIGHER PLANES OF EXISTENCE," illustrates the inherent, subtle conflicts between light and dark within each of us. The resonating power of symmetry and sacred geometry accentuate the variant shades of gray as an allusion to the "Shadow Self" that is often created to appease the public eye. The interlacing motifs represent the conscious and unconscious threads that constitute the fabric of individuals, and collectively as a species of sentient beings. The overall design also suggests an interconnected relationship with something eternal, out of time and greater than our selves. It is a reminder that in order to shed light onto, and ultimately excavate, our authentic selves, we must face the darkness unafraid.

Preface

"True wisdom comes to each of us when we realize how little we understand about life, ourselves, and the world around us."- Socrates

Chapter 1

The minute I saw the place I didn't like it! There was an eerie filthiness about it, suggestive of an abandoned time long ago. The sign out front said, "Emma's Chuck Wagon", but it didn't light up anymore. There were several decrepit pick-up trucks and a couple of old motorcycles out front. The whole pathetic building looked out of place, from a different time, and I wondered why it was still there. Bob told me to meet him at Denny's at this address, but this place didn't look like Denny's at all!

I promised to meet an old friend here for lunch. Bob moved to Los Angeles after high school, which is about a three hour drive from home. I don't go out of town that much and he doesn't either. So after several years of not seeing each other, we agreed to meet at some God forsaken desolate place in the middle of nowhere! At least we could have lunch together and catch up on our lives. Now I was thinking, "The middle of what?" I parked my car and went inside. Not surprising, there were six or seven people inside. Most were spread out across the establishment with two at each table. The exception was a peculiar lone wolf sitting at the lunch counter.

The cook behind the counter had all his attention meddling with something unseen. I couldn't determine if he was the waiter, dishwasher, or maybe the owner. There was a foreboding silence that seemed to linger on endlessly and became deafening the longer I stood there. The ancient wallpaper was dripping from the walls as if fighting to hold on during its final breaths of life. I was starting to come unglued!

I sat down at the bar a few seats from the lone wolf and waited for my friend to arrive. The place was a picture right out of the 1940's or early 50's. Something about the place didn't feel right. The air itself evoked a surreal and unnatural odor of time as if I'd disturbed a scene frozen long ago. Now that I was actually inside, it was even more unsettling.

The inside of the diner looked exactly as it must have looked the day it opened except for the years of crud built up in the crevices! There was stainless steel trim everywhere and a long counter with old-fashioned stools, attached to the floor. The counter was classic vinyl complete with a tiny steel border, secured with little nails. The grit collected in the crevices testified that it was all very old. Looking around at the tables, I was surprised they were still standing. Everything in the place was sixty or seventy years old. The whole place was a time capsule from another era and made me wonder why these people were even here. What was the attraction? They looked like regulars.

"Be right with you", the man behind the counter said, looking over his shoulder. His hair was saturated with cooking oil that sprayed like small geysers from the skillet before him.

"No problem", I said, "I'm waiting for someone for lunch."

I looked over at the guy sitting two stools down from me and watched as he stared silently into what looked like a big bowl of pea soup. Occasionally he would dip his spoon into the bowl, get a mouthful of soup and then continue staring ahead. His gaze was constant, unwavering in its determination. He appeared to be mesmerized by an invisible entity of which he was the only one privy to its esoteric and unspoken language. I tried not to stare at him, but he was very strange. He wore wire-rimmed glasses and had a head of gray hair that flowed everywhere at once and reminded me of a cross between Albert Einstein and Kramer from Seinfeld. Every now and then he'd look around the room, first to the left and then to the right. Then he would just stare straight ahead and keep slurping his soup.

The guy seemed consumed by some internal program. Completely lost in thought, periodically he would scribble something down, mumble a few words to himself, and then look straight ahead again. This went on for about fifteen minutes. I was getting a little anxious. I found myself continuously checking the front door, my watch, and this guy sitting at the counter with me. My friend was late!

"What'll ya have?" the guy behind the counter asked, appearing right in front of me snapping me out of a bad dream.

"Where's your friend?" Is he coming?" the waiter-cook guy asked.

"He's late. I'll have a cup of coffee while I wait." I said, glancing again at my watch.

"There comin you know!" the soup guys blurts out, as if patiently waiting for his moment to speak.

As I look in his direction, I was shocked to see him looking right at me! "Are you talking to me?" I said nervously.

"Course I'm talkin to you. You're right in front of me aren't you? You know why you're here don't you?" he asks, dipping another spoonful of soup and sticking it in his mouth.

"I'm here to meet a friend for lunch," I said.

9

"No, I mean why you're alive…. why you're here on earth?" he asked with a blank expectant look on his face.

"Wait. Do I know you? Who's coming? What are you talking about?" I asked, a little irritated that he was speaking to me like he knew me and yet… I suddenly felt very curious at what he was saying.

"The Caretakers are coming soon," he answered back staring directly into my eyes. "The end of all this is coming with them," he said as if he was making sense, as if he was somehow summarizing everything he had been saying and putting a point on it. Somehow this guy, this stranger, struck me as a very odd duck and I quickly became interested in whatever he had to say about anything. I moved over a couple of chairs to sit next to him and introduced myself.

"Hi, I'm Doug…. Doug Keller. What's your name?" I asked.

"My name's Jim, but they call me Dr. Frankenstein," he said with the slightest wry smile forming on his face as if he'd just remembered an old joke.

"Dr. Frankenstein? Why do they call you that? I asked. "Who calls you Dr. Frankenstein?" By now I was growing more and more curious. I was hooked and needed to better understand exactly who was sitting next to me at the lunch counter at Emma's.

"They call me that because I'm kind of a 'go-between' for the Caretakers and the rest of us. I'm what you might call electrical or conductive!" he said smiling with delight at revealing his secret knowledge. "I suppose in some way my work helps to bring life to dead things, you know, like Dr. Frankenstein!" he said, condescendingly as if his words held some secret brilliance.

"Who are the Caretakers?"

"UFOs, aliens, space people, you know….men from outer space! I don't know where they came from or when they came here. They picked me up about twenty years ago, and convinced me I needed to work with them. Well, they convinced me, so I do what they ask me to do," he said. "They actually do take care of us. They are brilliant creatures and very concerned about our development as a species. You wouldn't believe all the stuff they do and what they know," he said getting more and more excited. I could see that he was ready to pop!

I took a sip of my coffee and ordered a turkey sandwich. This guy sitting next to me was a full-blown wingnut! He was amazing! I was certain he'd drunk the cool aid a long time ago and asked for seconds. Maybe he saturated his brain so heavily with psychedelics that he now believes his hallucinations to be real. Being an amateur psychologist, I was intrigued by the depth and detail of this guy's delusions. I was fascinated and completely hooked. I needed to know more about the world this guy lived in and how he came to understand what he believed to be the truth. I took another sip of coffee and looked over at Jim…. at Dr. Frankenstein.

"What do you mean when you say they care about us?" I asked.

"Well, it's taken me a while to learn and to understand what they're doing and what they mean to do," Jim said taking a couple more slurps from his bowl which seemed to pull him instantly back to a calmer state.

"Jim, what exactly are they doing?" I asked.

"They gave us medicine and math. They help out from time to time with food crop issues, nudging civilization forward when it gets stuck. They study us and our behaviors. They help us to grow food better than we do. They drop hints for us when we're trying to develop new medicines or when we have a science problem," he said as if reciting from a history book.

"Do they have a spaceship?" I asked, with a subtle hint of sarcasm. A small spasm of guilt and shame shot through me for playing this pathetic guy like a trout but I couldn't help throwing out the question to see if he'd bite.

"Yes they have several spaceships. Actually they mostly live in the moon. Their home base is the moon and they use their spaceships to shuttle down and do their experiments," he said in a very straight-forward, matter of fact tone.

"They live in the moon?" I whispered almost choking on my coffee. "What do you mean they live on the moon?" This conversation was so wacky I was mentally searching my tackle-box for more lures for this guy.

"They actually live inside the moon. The moon is not really what we think it is. The moon is not a natural earth satellite. It was brought here by them a long time ago... before we were human... before humans were here on earth. They came here to grow a new life form. They came here to create us! They used the DNA that was already on the earth and made some changes to it, and presto! Here we are! They took DNA from the chimps and then changed it to produce a human being. Haven't you ever wondered why we've never found the missing link? There never was one!"

Even though I'd quit smoking years ago I suddenly felt the urge for a cigarette. This guy's delusional state was unbelievable! He had so much detail and utterly believed every single word. My mind was spinning with what I was hearing, and I was intrigued that he believed it all. By this time I had completely forgotten about meeting my friend for lunch. Something else was happening, and for what it was worth, I was going to follow it! Where did he come up with these ideas? How did he dream up all this stuff? How did he come to believe it to be real? I had to find out. I had to stick with this guy and get to the bottom of his story.

I snapped back from my internal dialogue and asked, "Why would they do that? What's in it for them? Why would they make us some kind of genetic experiment?" I asked.

"We have something they need!" he said almost in a whisper. "They figured out how to make us conscious! They gave us consciousness. It's what they want from us," he said with a face so serious he could have been looking down the barrel of a shotgun. He was dead serious! His intensity and piercing look unnerved me for a moment.

"You mean they don't want to eat us or take over our world or turn us into zombie slaves?" I replied thinking of the standard reasons of why aliens come to earth and attack us.

"No! They don't want to eat us. They control everything. They control the weather, earthquakes, tsunamis, hurricanes, everything!" he said. "Look. Here's what I've learned from these guys. They've been growing the population for centuries. The more people that are born, the greater the level of total human consciousness, but they don't take it until someone dies. Right before a person dies; they somehow collect or gather up that

13

person's total consciousness," he said in a whisper and crouching over my way sharing his secret knowledge.

"What do you mean by collect? How do they do that? And even if they could, why would they?" I asked growing more curious about what this all meant. My mind was exploding in a million directions struggling to understand what this all means.

"These guys have figured out a way to harness human consciousness as a material they use to keep the universe in balance. When someone dies the Caretakers are able to 'harvest' the deceased's consciousness. Somehow they can process it into a type of energy force they can direct to different parts of the universe to help maintain some kind of equilibrium or balance in the space-time continuum. It's their job as the Caretakers," he added. "They are the Caretakers of the universe...the whole universe!" Jim said gasping and giddy with the reality of what he was saying. "These are the creatures that make everything possible! They keep the universe in balance. They are truly amazing creatures and we don't have a clue!"

I wasn't in the mood for lunch anymore, but just then, the cook-waiter guy brought my turkey sandwich and fries. I needed a drink! I didn't believe a single word this guy was saying but he did. I don't know what inexplicable force kept me glued to the stool. I couldn't move! I couldn't leave. I couldn't just walk out on this guy and not find out the ending. How was this guy's story going to end? Everything he told me was burning me up inside. It was the craziest notion I'd ever heard. Yet, on some level, his story made sense, if that's even possible.

"So what do you do for them? How do you fit into their plan?" I asked.

"They say I have some kind of esoteric talent for comprehending divergent concepts in a way that allows me to visualize a variety of outcomes which they find useful when they need me to communicate with different people."

"Like who? What people do you communicate with?" I asked.

"Well, I talk to people, to anybody really. I just talk to anybody that will listen and tell them some of the crazy things swirling around in my head. Somehow, when I communicate this information, it gets downloaded into other people's unconsciousness and then it grows," he said in a matter of fact way as if he were teaching a class on the subject.

"Your job is to download information into human consciousness?" I asked beginning to interrogate him.

"Well, technically, it's the human unconscious, but yes! That's what I do. That's my role. That's my job with these guys. They rely on me to translate for them," Jim said as he finished up his bowl of soup. He looked down at his empty bow and then looked back at me and said, "Maybe translate is not the right word. It's more like an unconscious download."

"So are you 'downloading" some form of information to me right now?"

"No. We're just talking. I'm simply explaining what I do. I had a hunch that you might be someone who would find all of this interesting," he said looking at me like he was reassessing if he'd made the right decision in speaking with me.

"Well Jim, I don't know how to respond to what you've told me. I'm not sure I even understand what you've told me. What if I told someone all the stuff you've told me? What if I told the world the aliens were here?"

"Go ahead. I'm not worried about it. Do you realize what people will think when you tell them my story?" he said looking at me with that 'checkmate' look like he had outsmarted me.

I ate half my turkey sandwich and all of the fries and swallowed my last bit of coffee. I'm not sure what my mind was doing all this time. I was collecting myself, trying to put a little distance between me and him, trying to put the whole conversation in perspective, but I couldn't. I had to go!

"Well Jim, it's been nice talking to you," I said as I stood up and walked to the register. "You take care of yourself and good luck to you," I added.

"Yeah, it was nice talking to you too. Remember what I said about the end. It's coming soon," he commented as I walked away. He watched me walk over to the register and pay my bill. I headed for the front door and turned when I got there. He was watching me the whole time. I waved and he waved and I walked outside, back into the real world. That was the strangest lunch of my whole life!

I started my car and pulled out of the parking lot heading for the highway to return home. When I arrived home I realized that I had no conscious recollection of the entire drive home. I was there and then I was home. It seemed strange to me that I didn't remember the drive. There was so much to think about and I have no recollection of any of it. As I opened the front door and stepped in I immediately realized I wasn't alone. There was someone in my home! Turning on the light switch I looked around at my small apartment. Everything was there as I left it, exactly as I had left it. There was nothing strangely different at all. Then a weird feeling came over me like my home was too normal, too perfect the way I remembered it. What is this déjà vu feeling trying to tell me? What does it mean when something is so familiar you take it for granted?

I returned to my routine and my work schedule. The weeks passed, but I could not shake the nagging déjà vu feeling. It kept hanging on and coloring everything familiar to me. My life was somehow different now, but I didn't know how. Every little detail was as it's always been, as I clearly remember things to be. After three and a half weeks, I couldn't take it anymore, so I drove back down to Riverton to see if I could find Jim. As I made the turnoff onto the street where the café was I couldn't believe what I saw when I drove up! It wasn't there! Emma's Chuck Wagon was gone! Everything else was the same, but the building where Emma's had been simply wasn't there. Instead there was a Denny's. I double-checked my bearing, the landmarks, even the town, but this is the place… the exact place where I had lunch with Dr. Frankenstein!

Did I imagine the whole thing? Did something happen to me that made me forget… a bump on the head… too many beers… no sleep? Did I just dream this thing up and somehow it got loaded into what I rely on as my conscious self? Somehow Jim did something to me that changed everything. I felt a little dizzy and all of a sudden I was very hot. Sweating and gasping for air, the last thing I remember was trying to breathe.

When I woke up I was in my own bed back at home. How did I get here? What happened? What's happening to me? Just then, Jim came in and handed me a glass of water and said, "Here drink this. Your body needs liquids."

"Jim! What are you doing here? How did you get here? Where were you? What happened to Emma's? What's going on?" I pleaded with him for answers.

Jim just smiled and said, "I found you out in the backyard unconscious and brought you inside. What are neighbors for?"

"INNER TURMOIL | BLACK TEARS"

Chapter 2

I took a few days off from work to clear my mind. There were so many questions swirling in my head it felt like my whole life had entered a massive fogbank. My simple life had turned into a jigsaw puzzle with some of the pieces missing. Jim came over every day to make sure I was okay, which began to creep me out. However, it also gave me an opportunity to question him and to start putting the pieces of this mystery together. I had to find out what happened to me and Jim had the answers. Somehow I had unknowingly become part of something bigger than myself. I wasn't too sure what was going on, but my gut told me that I was in on this deal… the same deal that Jim was explaining back at Emma's.

"Jim, when did you become my neighbor and what the heck happened at Emma's?" I asked him the second day he came over.

"Well, it's like this Doug… I know… I mean they know, or they taught me how I could bend time and make things happen now… in the present, that won't manifest in time until tomorrow. What you thought was happening at Emma's last month actually hasn't even happened yet. Because of the way we can manipulate time, I can give you memories from the future. It's just easier that way. So I've been your neighbor for about two weeks, but you didn't know that because we haven't actually met at Emma's yet."

I began to see another side of Jim…a side I hadn't seen at Emma's. He had a simple kindness to him. He was strange, very strange, no doubt! But he also had a plain and simple way about him. The more he talked, the more I began to think of him as being elegantly simplistic and not bogged down with so many of the hang-ups most people have. He was laser focused on working with the aliens and doing what he does.

"That doesn't make any sense at all! It's complete bullshit! Are you trying to say that I don't know what I know… that I don't even know what's happening to me when it's happening?" I asked angrily. I was more unnerved now than before. Was I going crazy? Who the hell was this guy standing in front of me? Was he a crazy clown or just crazy? I couldn't tell.

"What I'm trying to tell you Doug, is that we have much to unlearn about who we are. What we've come to believe about ourselves, our history, and who we are as a species… it's wrong…it's incorrect. We mostly don't get it right and as a civilization. We are going in the wrong direction! Evolution is about to make a major correction to our path as a species," Jim stated patiently as if he was trying to console me.

"I don't get it. Okay, let's start again. Explain to me what you mean about all that time travel stuff you were babbling about," I said.

"Okay, I'll try. We humans believe that time moves in one direction… forward. We look back in time or we look forward in time. We have a recorded history of time and we have futurists who try to predict what will happen in the future. Are you with me so far?" Jim asked.

"Yeah, I'm with you."

"There are many laws in the universe that we have yet to discover. There's so much about the universe that we simply don't understand. We don't know how the whole universe works. We only have bits and pieces and theories. It's all connected. The universe is a single organism, if that's the right word for it. Do something over here and it affects something over there. When this happens... when anything at all happens... the act of it occurs "in time." It occurs over some period which we've come to call time. But in fact, everything happens instantly in the present. There is no time! It doesn't exist. It is an illusion that our mind uses to organize events. That's what I've been trying to tell you. The way our mind works is how we organize everything... our knowledge... our experience of things... and then we conclude that we have the truth about it. Our subjective experiences are magically transformed into our belief that it is "real." What we believe as fact is really an image created by our minds, but that is not really real. It's an image of what we believe is real. Objective knowledge is always subjectively perceived. That's the human filter," Jim explained.

"This is how the mind works. As it collects and stores present stimulation and converts it into data, the mind compares the new data to all past information as a kind of historical verification process to confirm its validity... and to properly organize it. What they've taught me about how our mind work is that, as we receive new data, it has an altering effect on all our historical data. It changes what we believe, what we've already learned, so it aligns more closely with what is happening in the present. As a result, it's possible to move human mental frames of reference very far very fast. The way our mind organizes everything lends itself automatically to change as we add new information. Depending upon the information, it's possible to change people's perspectives on everything very quickly," Jim explained.

"Yes, but if I haven't met you yet… if I'm not going to meet you at Emma's for another month… how do I know that now? Why do I have a memory of something that's never happened?" Jim just looked at me. I could tell he didn't have an answer to my question. This guy was a dipshit! He looks crazy! Why didn't I fully realize I was dealing with a crazy clown to begin with? Then I remembered that I did know it, but thought I could handle it. I was wrong!

"Uh, I'm not sure how you can recognize me from a meeting that hasn't happened yet. This is very strange. Doug, I haven't had this sort of thing happen before. I mean, I'm a kind of advance scout for the Caretakers. They send me out and I say what they've told me to say. At Emma's I was just being who I am. I wasn't on assignment. I wasn't recruiting you. How did you get all this information? How did you know what was going to happen and it hasn't even happened yet? Dude, you are freaking me out! I'm just the messenger. I don't have all the answers," Jim said.

I didn't have any answers for Jim. I was actually looking to him for the answers and it seemed he'd come up empty as well. Maybe he doesn't know as much as he thinks he does. Maybe he doesn't realize he's crazy! Hey, maybe I'm crazy too now! That actually makes sense! Why did I ever go into Emma's Chuck Wagon? I knew it wasn't right.

"Jim, I don't even know what's going on here. I don't remember you moving in next to me, but I do remember having lunch with you at Emma's in Riverton like it was yesterday… and thinking you were very strange."

Neither of us had an answer for what was happening to us. It felt like time was moving forward and backward at the same time as if we'd both been caught in a tide pool. Over the next few weeks, Jim explained a great many things to me about the Caretakers. He had been working with them for many years and how they had taught him many interesting facts about being human. They had explained the great value that humans bring to the universe. He also told me of the things he had learned, had paid attention to, and it sounded like he wasn't supposed to know. Many of the things he had seen and heard were never meant for him to see or hear. Because of this he knew much more than the Caretakers ever intended for him to know. All this information he shared with me for whatever reason. Maybe he needed to unburden himself of such knowledgeable things... of such incredible things.

During such conversations I came to understand a deeper aspect of Jim. He was alone. He had been an essential part of this operation for many years, but he was basically alone in the world. I sensed he was reaching out to me in friendship, maybe to avoid his solitude and also, maybe to help him shoulder his burden. I wasn't his replacement, but I was someone who could walk with him down the path that had been chosen for him. I wondered if I could be friends with Jim.

What I had learned about the Caretakers, what Jim had told me so far was this: they had come here a long time ago...a very long time ago. They've been here for about a million years and maybe a little more. They were sent here by their race or their leader to help our world develop into what it is today. They were sent to make sure that the human race made it...that we developed into the creatures we are today. There was so much detail... so many different ways they intervened, supported, and nudged us toward full consciousness. I remember Jim telling me at Emma's how the Caretakers could somehow harvest a person's consciousness and use it for some purpose, in some way that somehow helps the whole universe.

Then I remembered this conversation, "Doug, what I've learned from them is this… human consciousness is something that is not that common. After we die, our consciousness continues, but in a slightly different way. Somehow we become connected to all other human consciousness, into a sort of unified single consciousness. This unified entity helps the universe manage itself, if that's the right word. It's more like our consciousness keeps the universe in a suspended state, a more stable state of being."

"How do you know this Jim? Have you seen it?"

"No, I've only heard the Caretakers discussing different aspects of it," he said.

"Have you been to their base on the moon?" I asked almost not believing that I was asking that question.

"No I haven't," was his reply. "I've only been to some of their locations here on earth and been in one of their spacecraft several times."

"You were in their spaceship?" I asked in disbelief when I realized what we were talking about. Immediately I was shocked at my level of acceptance of our conversation. I had immersed myself in Jim's delusions to the point that I had begun accepting them as normal subjects of our conversations.

"Yeah, it was when they first recruited me. I was living in Los Angeles and driving to Las Vegas when my car broke down about thirty miles outside of Barstow. I was waiting for a tow truck when the next thing I knew there they were! Then, all of a sudden I was in some kind of craft. It was sort of dreamlike and for a long time I thought that I had imagined it. It seemed so real and I remember being able to see out of the ship like the whole thing was transparent. I could see us flying over the ocean and I think we went to Tibet. I think they have a big base somewhere in Tibet."

I sat there completely spellbound by what Jim was telling me. Part of me wanted to believe him. I wanted to believe this was really real, really happening. My scientific side said I needed proof.

"Jim, do you remember where in Tibet they took you?" I asked. "Hey, why do you think you were in Tibet?" I asked, feeling suspicious about this whole story.

"No. I only remember that it was cold when we went outside briefly and then we went a very long ways down into the earth. I think it must have been miles and miles down. When we left the ship, it looked like a whole city was down there."

"How did you know you were in Tibet?" I asked again.

"Oh, because we could see the huge mountains below covered in snow," he answered.

"Was there a tunnel, a cave, an opening? How could they hide such a place from the rest of us?" I asked.

"It was very strange. I remember that it seemed like we flew right into the side of a cliff! I thought we were going to crash, but we sort of slowed down and there was this humming sound, and then, we just flew into the cliff like it wasn't even there! The next thing I knew, we were somewhere deep inside the mountain. It was as if the rock wasn't even there, like the ship was making its own tunnel or shaft!"

"I was there for what seemed like a couple of days and then we left. I don't know how long I was there. There's no time when you are with them. You're just there. I think when I go with them we enter something like a parallel dimension. Then they took me to another place, another one of their bases. This time I clearly remember seeing the Pyramids and we flew right into the Sphinx! I think their base inside the Sphinx is their headquarters on earth. What I learned while I was there is that they built it! They built the Sphinx and also the Pyramids. I don't know how long I was there. They didn't say very much to me. They didn't probe me or do any experiments on me or anything like that. It was more like they were just letting me watch what they were doing. Before we left the Sphinx, one of them approached me and spoke to me in English."

"What did he say?" I asked. By this time I was again fully involved, intrigued and needing to know all the details.

"He was very large; the largest of them that I had seen. Most all of them looked like regular people, but this one was probably seven feet tall and very muscular! He said his name but I couldn't pronounce it. I couldn't even remember the sound he made when he spoke it, so he said to just call him Gabe. Gabe told me that they were not people from this planet, but they were here to help us, to help humanity become fully aware. He said there were many things we still did not understand about the cosmos and they were here to help us to grow… to learn… to understand… and to eventually evolve into what he termed, "the full potential of our being." That's what he said to me. Gabe said that I should not be afraid of them, that no harm

27

would come to me. He said that I had been selected to work with them because I had a kind heart and a clear conscious which helps them to download information into the collective unconscious."

"What the hell is the collective unconscious? Are you trying to tell me that somehow we all have the same brain or something like ESP?" I asked. I had the sense that Jim was making this up and couldn't fathom how any of it could be true. Jim really was crazy! I began to get this sinking feeling that I was crazy now too or at least, I was going crazy!

"Doug, our psychologists and scientists have known for a long time that there is a connection between people... a connection that does not always make sense. It's a kind of ESP talent that has not been fully developed in our species yet. The Caretakers explained that all conscious humans share a vast pool of something called the collective unconscious. I can't explain how it works or why it exists, but it does. Every single person can learn to access it. Somehow, during our lives, we inadvertently make deposits to the collective unconscious. It's like our minds are tape recorders and that information goes somewhere. It streams into the collective unconscious where it can be 'tapped' or used by another individual. It's all true! The problem is we don't believe this stuff anymore," Jim explained.

"Some of us have been selected to serve as custodians to the human race by allowing new information to be inserted into this collective unconscious. That's why some of the stuff I know I can't explain. I don't know where it comes from. I simply have it in my consciousness for a while and then it's gone. But once it's been introduced into the human unconscious through me, then it becomes available to everyone living in the world. It may be an idea, a feeling, a concept, a notion that their minds can begin to work on and develop. At some point, BINGO! Someone has a major breakthrough when their mind figures out what to do with that information. That's how they do it!" he said with a look of finality and relief on his face.

I wanted to believe Jim. I really wanted to believe the idea that we were being helped by someone bigger or smarter than us. I never believed in God or religion or any of that stuff. Part of me was being pulled into Jim's story hoping we weren't really alone in the cosmos, and something else was going on with me. I was looking for a scientific angle to this mystery. I've always been fascinated by astronomy and space and science. The space stuff always seemed way beyond my ability to comprehend... to fully understand it. But I loved it all anyway! I loved everything that I could understand and even what I could imagine. I loved Star Trek! I loved Star Wars! I loved every space show and space movie that was ever made and now I was talking with a guy that says he's part of their team. He's telling me they are real! I wish I could believe him.

"Jim, can you take me to see them? I asked. This would be the test.

"I don't know. I can ask them next time they contact me, but they usually arrange those things. I've been working with them for about twenty years and they've never used me to bring someone to them. Besides, it's not that easy. When they contact me, I never know when or where I'll be... like the first time when I was outside Barstow on my way to Vegas. Remember when I said that I thought I'd been gone for several days? Well, after all that traveling, I ended up back in my car on the side of the road. I must have fallen asleep because the tow-truck driver honked his horn and woke me up. He fixed my car and I was on my way," Jim explained.

"The wire to the alternator had come off, and my battery was dead. He fixed it and charged my battery, Then, I was back on the road. For a long time I thought that somehow maybe I had dreamed the whole thing, but my mind could never let go of the details. I had seen too much. Also, when I was in the place in Tibet, I scraped my arm on a rock. When I woke up in my car, there was a scab on my arm where I remembered scraping it. It all seemed so strange and weird and confusing at first. After a few years of living through these experiences, I came to understand what was happening to me. But I can't take you to see them. If they want to see you… they'll come for you themselves!" he said.

Eventually I went back to work, back to my real life…. to a more normal life. For the next few weeks or so I would see Jim four or five times a week and we would talk about his adventures with the aliens. The more and more I got back into my routine, the more I realized there was something seriously wrong with Jim. He seemed to be a normal person, not crazy, not violent or anti-social. On the contrary, he was friendly and outgoing and I would see him sometimes talking with our neighbors and they seemed to interact with him in a normal way, in a neighborly way. I knew he was crazy, but part of me really wanted to believe his story. A part of me needed to know that aliens really existed and were friendly. Part of me wanted to believe they were here to help the whole world.

I had come to think of Jim as a friend. We had developed so much common ground in our brief relationship. I believed him to be a very caring person, but also, someone that was

30

deranged…mentally unstable. He really believed all the things he was telling me. There had to be something to what he was saying because I had experienced some of it, but didn't know what it meant. Was I going crazy? Was I starting to live in Jim's world? I didn't know anymore.

Somehow this whole story held out a small sliver of hope for me. I wanted to believe it was possible that the fate of the world was not entirely in the hands of selfish little men that controlled countries, economies, and nuclear weapons. But then, I knew it wasn't true. I knew that Jim was crazy and that the entire human race would have to work out their own problems and hoped nobody pulled the trigger. Still, I held out hope that there were actual Caretakers that protected us from ourselves.

A few weeks after Jim found me in my back yard unconscious, my friend Bob called me. Bob and I had been high school friends until he moved away about ten years ago. He said he really needed to see me, but couldn't get away for a weekend visit and couldn't we meet somewhere between? Bob lived about three hundred miles from me and so I agreed to meet him in Riverton for lunch. He gave me the address of the restaurant and it was a date. It seemed silly to me now thinking about going back to Riverton after all the stuff I'd gone through and meeting Jim and all. It seemed laughable. I was set to meet Bob in Riverton on Saturday at 11 AM.

Hearing Bob's voice reminded me of our high school days. We were best friends. We were nerds! Neither of us played football, baseball, or basketball. We didn't do any sports at all for that matter. Bob and I were science guys…more specifically science fiction guys and computer geeks. The hard part for me was that I wasn't as smart as Bob when it came to math and physics, two essentials for geeks. All our friends were straight A students in these subjects, as was Bob. I struggled to earn a B in those subjects. The three areas where I excelled were computers, biology, and physiology. I'm not sure how I learned computer programming, but when I did, it came naturally to me. It was probably my insatiable desire to want to make machines do things they never did before and to fully understand how they worked. Computers are my specialty! It wasn't until my third year at college that I finally mastered the math and physics that would serve me later in life. College was where I became acquainted with the study of genomics. It was love at first sight!

As I pulled into the parking lot, the strangest feeling came over me. I felt like I had been here before. The sign said, "Emma's Chuck Wagon!" The last time I was here, there was a Denny's right here on this very spot… the very spot where I had met Jim… where I was supposed to meet Bob. I knew all this stuff before I came here and thought it was all so not true and now here I am waiting for Bob at Emma's Chuck Wagon just like I remembered it.

I walked into the restaurant and it was exactly like it was before and there was Jim sitting there exactly like before. I sat at the counter and ordered a coffee, knowing that Bob would not be coming to join me. And then Jim started talking to me like he had done before. Jim didn't seem to know me… but maybe he did. I knew what he was going to say before he said it. I knew what was going to happen before it happened! Everything played out exactly like it had the first time, a month ago, or just now! How can something occur exactly the same way two times in a row? I don't know. I only know… that I think I know what comes next, but not really sure about anything anymore!

When I got back home I made an appointment to see a psychiatrist. I knew there was something seriously wrong with me. Over the next several months, Dr. Jameson helped me to understand some of the things that had happened to me. Part of my problem had been a chemical reaction with some of my medications, specifically my Lexapro, Nyquil, and Ambien, mixed with alcohol. There were too many chemicals floating around in my system. It was affecting my brainwaves. The other part of the equation involved my work and stress and poor diet and lack of exercise, and something else as well. At one point in my treatment, Dr. Jameson insisted that I have an MRI to scan my brain. The MRI turned up an old injury, a slight trauma to the medulla oblongata that I had sustained at some point in the past. It may have been nothing, but it may also have contributed to my hallucinations. After four months of treatments, Dr. Jameson felt I was better and didn't need to see him anymore. It felt like a very strange chapter in my life was over and I could finally move on.

I hadn't seen Jim at all since I got back from Riverton. The house where he was living was empty. There was no one living in it now. I asked the neighbors about "Jim" but they didn't know anyone by that name that had lived in the house. They said the man that used to live there got transferred and left a few days ago. I thought it was odd and maybe coincidental, but I let it go. I was cured! I was all better and back at my old life now. Still, there was a part of me that missed him. I had come to like him even if he had problems.

Jim had opened my eyes to some new possibilities about life…about the world we live in. I had accepted all the textbook lessons of history like most people do. I had never questioned my cultural values and had accepted the problems of the world as mostly unsolvable. Suddenly I began to realize how very little I actually knew about anything! Like most people, it was better for me to focus on my own goals and the things that mattered most to me. That's pretty much how I felt before I met Jim. Now....everything is different for me. I miss Jim... even if he was crazy!

"YOU SHALL ATONE"

Chapter 3

The minute I saw her I fell in love! I've never believed in love at first sight, but then it happened to me just like that! It was her first day on the job and as I walked into the break room to grab a cup of coffee, she was standing there pouring herself a cup of coffee. She was an angel! When I saw her standing there I was speechless. She looked up at me and offered to pour me a cup.

"Yes. Thank you!" I stammered. I felt completely naked and vulnerable in front of her. She didn't seem to notice my embarrassment or herculean efforts to control my emotions.

"You're welcome! My name is Mary," she said with a brilliant smile.

"Hi, I'm Doug," I said trying to be calm. "I work in research. How long have you been with the company? I asked, trying to regroup and put a little distance between us. The small talk seemed to help.

"Today's my first day. I'm excited to be here and to be working again. This seems like a great company," she said.

"It is a great company. I've been here for about five years and still find the work challenging," I replied. "What department do you work in?" I asked.

"I work in personnel," she answered. "I've got to get back to work. Nice meeting you Doug," she said as she walked off.

"Likewise," I said feeling like I'd dodged a bullet. I was in love! I was smitten by this woman! How could this be happening to me so soon after all the weird stuff with the aliens and Jim? I hope she likes me. The shock of the arrow right through my heart didn't wear off! The next four or five days made me crazy all over again. I'd hang around the break room hoping to bump into Mary. I'd lay awake at night feeling all alone for the first time in my life. I never believed in love at first sight! I guess I was wrong.

Within a week I couldn't stand it anymore. I overcame my fear and asked Mary out. She accepted! I was thrilled! We went to a very nice restaurant. Afterwards we walked around in the park across the street and talked. I learned that Mary had just moved to town because she had gotten the job with my company. She was single and had graduated from college with a degree in human resources and a minor in religion. She was Catholic and had briefly considered becoming a nun, but decided it wasn't for her. Mary said she wanted to have children someday. I could tell by the way she looked at me that it was love at first sight with her as well.

We continued to date for almost a year when I decided to pop the question:

"Will you marry me?" I asked.

"Absolutely yes!" Mary replied.

We were married and within a year we had our first child. Justin was seven pounds four ounces at birth and was the very best thing that ever happened to us until Doug Junior came along only the next year weighing in at seven pounds six ounces at birth. Life was so good with Mary and my two boys. I had never mentioned anything to Mary about my psychiatrist visits or Jim and Emma's Chuck Wagon. I didn't need to. That was ancient history now. I was a family man and happily married to the most wonderful woman in the world. I hadn't heard from Jim since I'd met Mary. Good! My life was better now.

During our courtship I made several clandestine trips to Riverton to ease my mind of the nagging details from Emma's and to make sure I wasn't really crazy or caught up in some strange tale. It was my way of maintaining my sanity, even if it was slightly obsessive-compulsive. Every time I went there I pulled into the same Denny's restaurant and ordered a cup of coffee to go and came home. I had to walk inside to make sure it was really there and that I wouldn't walk into Emma's again. The whole memory of Emma's morphed into a strange and surreal nightmare that lingered on inside me unattached to anything. I was relieved that episode was behind me and my life was back on track with a beautiful wife and two wonderful boys. Looking into the future I could see us playing baseball and going on picnics and to the zoo, just the four of us.

About three months after Doug Junior was born, I received a promotion to department head. The promotion came with a very nice salary increase and included a company car and... a bigger office! It also meant that I would need to travel from time to time. I always hated leaving Mary and the kids, but the job paid well, we were saving money, and someday my kids would need the money for college. It felt like my life was settling down into a natural flow of time and it was all good.

The trips were never that long, maybe two to three days at the most, but it was unbearable to be away from my family. Every now and then while I was away, I'd have a nightmare and wake up in the middle of the night in a dark hotel room and wonder if I was dreaming. It always took me a couple of minutes to focus and realize I was in a hotel room…that I was dreaming. It was only a dream! The dreams always felt real. I'd drift off to sleep and then wake up in Egypt by the Pyramids or in Tibet on a mountainside and then I'd wake up in my hotel room again. These dreams didn't happen often, but when they did, they were frightening. They reminded me of Jim's story and his tale of aliens and spaceships.

My life with Mary and the boys was more than I had ever hoped or expected. I'm not sure what others expect, but clearly my expectations had been too small. Everything Mary did was wonderful. She was a sweet nurturing mother to the boys and a great wife to me. Ever since my promotion, Mary didn't need to work, so she quit to stay home and raise our children.

When the boys were born she insisted they be baptized into the Catholic Church. I knew going into this marriage that Mary had very strong religious beliefs, so it wasn't a surprise to me when she asked that they be baptized. I didn't mind as long as she was happy. I never cared much for any of the religion stuff, but she did and my boys did. Besides, the people at the church were very nice. Church life became part of our family life. I went to church every Sunday with my wife and boys and felt good that they were getting some structure in their life. It didn't matter to me that I didn't really believe any of it.

The trouble started one day when Mary asked me about my own baptism and I told her I had never been baptized. "My family wasn't religious!" I said in an exasperated tone. "It just wasn't important to us. Hey, I don't throw rocks and stone when it comes to that kind of stuff! I don't care what other people believe. I just don't happen to believe any of it." I said defensively.

"Doug, you know there is a God that loves you," Mary said, putting her hand on her hips and looking at me like she was mother superior. She had such a calm and peaceful way of asserting herself. When Mary set her mind to a task there was no stopping her.

"Mary, we've been through this stuff before. I have the greatest respect for you and your religion. I understand it and accept it. I realize how important it is for our boys to grow up believing in something bigger than them. I just haven't gotten to a point yet, where I can believe all that stuff is real. Hey, I'm a scientist. I need proof! Its' just not real for me," I said hoping she'd let the whole thing go. She wasn't going to do that.

"Doug, it's very important to me that you are baptized. It may not be important for you, but it is for me, and for our two sons," she said, with a pleading look I couldn't resist.

"Mary, if it's that important to you, then, let me think about it for a while. If I decide to do this, I want it done in private. I'm not going up there in front of the whole congregation," I said and I meant it!

"Fine, we'll talk about it later." she replied.

We didn't talk about it later. We didn't talk about it for months. It seemed every time the subject came up, we were interrupted and then never got back around to it. I was fine with that. I hadn't changed my mind one bit. On the one hand, it didn't mean anything to me, so if I did it, I'd just be doing it for Mary and the boys. On the other hand, my heart wasn't in it. I didn't believe it and part of me felt like a hypocrite if I went through with it. A man has to stand on principle sometime.

It wasn't until my mother's death that I had any more thoughts about baptism. My mom had been a happy person all her life. Even after dad had died she seemed to bounce back and get back into living her life. She was a simple woman with very simple needs. And she was always happy. She loved Mary and the kids and enjoyed spending time with us as much as she was able. Her death changed me. I had thought about her death and imagined it, many times after my dad died. While it was painful to imagine, living through it was much more than I had I could ever have imagined. I realized that my mom occupied a bigger part of my heart than I had believed. I realized that life can bring a depth of pain and grief that can't be imagined. This personal knowledge of death and the changes it brings into people's lives was a reminder to me. It felt like part of me died with my mother. I had a beautiful wife and two wonderful boys, but life wasn't the same after my mom died. In some strange way I felt alone in the world now.

Maybe that's what started me thinking about baptism. Maybe that's what started me rethinking this whole God thing. After about three months after my mom died, I told Mary that maybe I should get baptized. I still wasn't completely convinced, but I needed something to be more closely connected to the only family I had left. So I agreed to be baptized. It was a quiet and private ceremony, with only my wife and two boys present, but I did it. I got baptized. I didn't feel any different afterwards, but accepted the rosary and agreed to wear it every day as a memorial to my mom. Maybe this would help my grief and sense of separation. It seemed to help me feel closer to my mom and to Mary and the boys. I learned a painful lesson from my mother's death: our family is the greatest asset we will ever have in this life!

"CITTA-SAMATANA | THE MINDSTREAM"

Chapter 4

A few months after my baptism, I got a phone call from Bob. He said his life was going well. He was married with three children of his own. I told him about Mary and our two boys and about my promotion. We talked for a while, compared schedules, and tried to work out a weekend where our two families could get together and where we could spend a little time together. It seemed like we both had the same problems- pre-school, elementary school, church functions, family commitments, and deadlines on the job. There didn't seem to be any time for old friendships. The funny thing was Bob asked if we couldn't at least have lunch together some Saturday and suggested we could meet in Riverton. We both laughed.

"Bob, you've stood me up once already. That whole thing has cost me way more than you know. Can't we make it someplace else?"

"Doug, Riverton is exactly halfway between us. I promise I'll be there this time,"

 I agreed that we'd meet the following Saturday in Riverton at the Denny's. I was very familiar with the Denny's in Riverton by this time, but wasn't going to bring that up to anyone.

I told Mary about my phone call with Bob. She had never met Bob, but knew of him from our conversations and knew we had been friends from high school. I told her I was going to drive to Riverton on Saturday next and have lunch with him. She thought that would be a great idea and asked if I wouldn't talk to him about maybe getting our families together sometime. I explained that we had been trying, but both of us have not been able to find the time. I assured Mary I would see what we could come up with a date for a family outing.

On Saturday, I gave my wife a kiss and hugged my boys before I left for Riverton. Finally Bob and I were going to get together and talk about old times and get reconnected. So much has happened to both of us over the years and it will be fun to see how he's changed and what he looks like now. I wanted to see the pictures of his wife and kids and can't wait to show him photos of my family. I also wanted to hear all about his career and what type of research he was working on.

I made the turnoff into Riverton and pointed the car down Main Street toward the Denny's like I always did. When I turned into the parking lot the blood drained from my body! I felt dizzy and wanted to vomit! It was Emma's Chuck Wagon parking lot! There was nothing to do now but go inside. Part of me was wondering if Bob would show up, but I doubted it. I went inside and took a seat: my usual seat at the counter. The place was empty, completely empty, except for the guy behind the counter. He wasn't the same guy. I ordered a cup of coffee and waited for whatever was going to happen next. It wasn't long before someone else did enter the restaurant. He sat at the counter about two stools down from me and ordered a coffee. I knew he was there to meet me.

He took a sip of his coffee and turned to me.

"My name is Micah and I believe we have a lunch date."

"Actually, I'm waiting for my friend Bob to arrive. I'm supposed to be having lunch with Bob," I said.

"Bob isn't coming today. This meeting was arranged for me to meet you and to show you around. Are you ready?"

"Show me around? Am I ready? No! I'm not ready. I'm not ready for any of this crap! I've been off drugs for years and thought this was just a dream. I'm not ready at all!" And with that Micah and the guy behind the counter grabbed me and took me in the back room. This is where things got a little fuzzy. I remember them opening up the walk-in door and all three of us going inside. I remember Micah shutting the door. Instantly it was no longer a walk-in cool box in a restaurant... but what seems to be the inside of a spaceship. It felt very strange and I felt strange as Micah and the cook morphed into these different kinds of beings right in front of me. They seemed human enough and friendly, but they weren't who they had appeared to be.

"We're going on a voyage Doug. It's time for you to begin your training. Jim led us to you and once he'd made contact with you, we knew you were the one we've been looking for," Micah said looking at me like he'd known me for a long time.

"Where are we going?" I asked. Before they could answer, I said, "Tibet?"

"No Doug, we're not going to Tibet."

"Egypt?" I blurted out, feeling contempt for these guys and also an overwhelming fear that my nightmares had been real all along.

"No Doug. We're not going to Egypt," Micah replied.

"Well, where are we going then?" I yelled back at him.

"You'll find out soon enough!" Micah said, with a slight smile.

His answer sent a chill down my spine and fueled my already growing fear. Then I laughed to myself…realizing my complete helpless in this situation. I looked around the room as everything began to light up and noticed I could see right through the walls of the craft. I could see outside and realized we were already several miles above the earth. It was breathtaking! I couldn't feel us moving at all. For all I could feel, we were still in the cool box at Emma's except I could see clearly that we weren't!

I watched as the earth got smaller and smaller. I could see it just hanging in space suspended in the darkness surrounding it. It gave me a funny feeling to see the world from so far away. It felt like the earth was an eternity away and my life was long gone. My thoughts turned to Mary and my boys. *What would happen to them? What would happen to me?* I missed them and only wanted to go home to them. I wanted to wake up and have this thing over with. Without realizing it, I had unconsciously grabbed the rosary around my neck and only now realized I was clutching it. In some strange way, it gave me comfort in this situation. Silly superstition and yet, holding it, I felt my mom's presence. It connected me to my family back on earth.

The moon grew larger and larger right in front of my eyes. I had never seen it so close before. It was huge! And it was bright…very bright. It's not the creamy whitish yellow color we see from earth. The moon was a silver colored brilliant giant disc reflecting back from the surface….almost like a mirror. It wasn't long before the moon covered all horizons and I realized where they were taking me. We were descending right into the moon when I heard a humming sound! We traveled some distance below the surface, but I don't know how far down we went.

"It's time for us to depart now. You will begin your time of study on the moon and what you learn here you must keep secret. All of humanity depends upon your silent understanding of what you will soon learn." Micah explained. I had no idea what he was talking about. I was hoping I would wake up and this bad dream would be gone.

When we left the ship we entered another world. It was a complete world with sunlight and mountains and trees! There were birds flying and a beach with an ocean and...something unimagined...the moon had an atmosphere! Everything was different here. The birds were not like any birds I had ever seen. The fish were different too and in ways hard to describe. Even Micah looked different now. He seemed taller, larger, and more powerful. His skin was more colorful, an almost metallic bronze color. We walked a ways up a beach and then into the forest. It wasn't hot and it wasn't cold, and there was a slight breeze blowing. It felt perfect! The air felt like it should feel all the time. I followed Micah down a trail on the forest floor. The path was about ten feet wide and on either side were trees and vegetation. We walked for what seemed like a half a mile when we came to a clearing in the forest. I could see about three hundred yards across the clearing to where the trees began again. In the clearing were several huts of many shapes and sizes.

We entered a small building through a narrow door that opened into a magnificent room. It was as if sunlight was streaming in, but from where? We were on the inside of the moon! The interior of the building was intriguing. I couldn't determine if it was Egyptian or Gothic! Can there be such a thing as Gothic Egyptian? If so, then this was it! Portions of the room were simple geometric shapes constructed of stone. Two of the walls were carved with what appeared to me to be Egyptian hieroglyphs. Other parts of the interior were made in such a way suggesting gothic spires with columns and archways one might find in a Gothic church. The proportions to the room did not match at all. I estimated the ceiling to be thirty feet tall at a minimum.

"Wait here!" Micah said, and walked off. When he returned he was accompanied by a very large and intimidating creature. When I first saw him I was unnerved. Never had I been in the presence of someone so physically imposing! This man or whatever he was carried a powerful vibe that was impossible to ignore.

"Doug, this is Gabe. He will be your teacher in this place."

"Hi Doug, how are you?" Gabe said. When he spoke, his voice sounded like a waterfall. It reminded me of the sound of thunder and the wind at the same time. I had never heard a human voice sound like that. It was terrifying.

"I'm, I'm fine. Thank you," I said feeling a wave of fear pour over me. Gabe's physical presence was overwhelming! He was massive! His whole being radiated energy or light or something. It was as if he didn't move at all and everything moved around him. I couldn't take my eyes off him!

"Doug, you are here to learn many things. You will come to understand who we are and why we are here. You are here to also learn about who you are and what role you will play in the coming changes on earth," Gabe explained all the while peering at me through crystal blues eyes set deep in his massive head. The only thing I could compare him to is the statue of David, but alive and walking and talking.

"What do you mean the coming changes?" I asked, trying to dig up the energy to speak up.

"There will be time for you to understand all these things. Come, let's eat and we can talk while we eat," Gabe said.

We walked outside the building and about two hundred yards down a trail. There before us was a table spread out with a variety of foods. Gabe and I sat down and we began to eat and talk. "Can I ask you a question Gabe?" I asked.

"You can ask me anything Doug," he replied.

"Where are you from and why are you here on earth? Do you know Jim? Was Jim real? Why am I here? What do I have to do with any of this? When can I go home?" Once I opened my mouth I couldn't stop asking questions. Gabe just looked at me and laughed.

"I will answer all your questions, but only one at a time. First, I am from a time long ago. Some of us have been here since the beginning. We are Caretakers and stewards of the universe. It is our job to care for all life and to help when help is needed. We have been watching and helping your planet from the very beginning. We were here when it was a molten rock. My kind forged the foundations of the world and shaped its celestial structure. We are ancient terra formers Doug! We watched the dinosaurs come and go and millions of different species of plants and animals in between. We've watched your planet change and evolve to become what it is today," Gabe explained.

"I don't understand how that's possible. I can't imagine what it must be like to live that long. I've never known someone so old. How can you do what you do? How can you be so old?" I asked.

"I am not old Doug. I am ancient. I am immortal!" he replied.

I had been so focused on Gabe and what he was saying and what I was hearing, I hadn't noticed that we were not alone. There were many different people around us and strange creatures as well. Some were flying creatures with great wings and others seemed almost human. There were other creatures as well, but I don't know how to describe them. There were creatures filled with eyes that looked in several directions at the same time. There were creatures that looked like people, but had wings and flew or seemed to hover. Actually, many of the creatures I was seeing didn't seem to move with any effort at all. It was as if they floated from place to place in some sort of animation like floating in water. Being on the moon and all, I was still surprised to accept such a multitude of new life forms with mild curiosity. My mind had arrived at a place where I believed anything was possible!

"Now to your friend Jim," Gabe said, snapping me back into the conversation. "Jim has been part of our program for many years now. He has been very helpful in shuttling information into the human unconsciousness stream," Gabe shared.

"Jim was recruited to help with your download, just as you suspected. He helped us to link into your subconscious and to establish the connection to you. Much of what you have already learned was given to you in this way," Gabe explained.

"The human unconsciousness stream; what is that exactly?" I said, staring at Gabe and noticing again how really huge he was. He was like a gigantic lion or bear, but morphed into a human-like appearance. His skin seemed to shimmer and glow. I felt disconnected like I was outside myself watching this scene from a surreal dream. Whatever Gabe was doing at the moment was what he was supposed to be doing. His every movement or word commanded a focused attention. His actions made me think of planets moving around the sun as they must do.

"The human unconsciousness stream is simply a term we use to describe the intricate unconscious connections that connect a local human consciousness with all other human unconsciousness. Have you ever wondered where ideas come from?" Gabe asked.

"Not really. I always thought that ideas kind of popped into our head." I shared.

"Well, they do pop into your head, but this only happens when your conscious and unconscious parts of your mind connect and create a doorway from one world to the other. A thought is either conscious or unconscious. Did you ever dream that you could think unconscious thoughts?" Gabe asked.

"I never really thought about it much," I replied.

"Well, you do and everyone does, and part of our job is to keep human consciousness focused on a program of continued development of more and more sophisticated thought forms. We keep introducing more highly evolved ideas that nurture your species to develop deeper mental and emotional capabilities. Humans are approaching a time when you will no longer need to speak words to communicate. Of course it will be hundreds of more years, but you are getting close. Some of your species are able to do this now!" Gabe explained.

"Your psychologists, psychiatrists, doctors, and scientists seem to think you have human consciousness figured out, but you don't. You're not even close! Your whole scientific community is convinced that the statistical method will always yield accurate data. Sometimes it does and sometimes it does not! Science has become blind to the unique qualities of the individual specimens being studied. Specifically, scientific studies are interested in averaging individual events. It minimizes any single data point as irrelevant to the validity of the overall results. Your logic tells you that this process is always accurate because it usually is, given the subject matter you are examining. The problem is-it doesn't work with people; more specifically it is not a valid tool when working with any aspect of the individual human consciousness. The process can't effectively capture the uniqueness of the individual being studied." Gabe stopped talking and just looked at me. He was studying me to determine if I understood what he had just said.

"I hear what you are saying Gabe, but I'm not sure I understand how it applies. I'm not sure what you are getting at. Can you explain it to me in a different way?" I asked.

"Doug, every physical human brain is wired about the same way, not exactly, but similar. When you cancel out all things that are similar, you are left with several other factors that must be considered when studying any one person. For example, everyone's DNA is different. It's a small difference, but there is a difference. It's a difference that must be considered and must be factored into the equation. There is also cerebral cell structure, the way the neural networks are formed, and the health of those networks. Another factor that almost never gets considered is that each human brain generates electricity. Some brains generate much more electricity than others. That is a huge factor when considering any statistical sampling, but nobody seems to talk about these differences. There is also the dynamic issue of neural plasticity. Your psychologists are only now beginning to understand the infinite variables that the neural plasticity dynamic presents. It's a different dynamic for each person."

I was beginning to see where Gabe was going with this topic, but not exactly sure where we would end up.

Gabe continued," So far Doug, we've just been talking about the human brain, which has its own set of problems and solutions. We haven't even begun to discuss the human mind yet. The mind is completely different than the brain. It's not the same thing at all!" he stated rather emphatically.

"What do you mean?" I asked.

"Have you ever seen a mind? Some people believe they don't exist. Some people believe a human mind is a by-product of chemical reactions in the brain that produce a residual effect of human consciousness that appears to reside someplace we call, for lack of a better term, the human mind. The human mind doesn't exist technically in any of the three dimensions that human scientists have come to rely on. It's there, but it's not there. Kind of like a Higgs Boson!" he said.

"What's a Higgs Boson?" I asked.

"It's a small, but essential part of the universe that exists for very short periods of time, but it's also a necessary and critical part of everything that is. We need the Higgs Boson for the universe to stay together and to hold all the physical properties together in an elegant whole system. The human mind is very similar to that!" Gabe said, staring at me with a look that said he was expecting me to be downloading all this information he was sharing. I was trying to understand.

"Now Doug, we're getting to the best part, the most interesting part of this whole equation. Engineering human consciousness was not terribly difficult. Consciousness breeds consciousness. Where did human consciousness begin? It's a very good question! Very soon, you humans will be able to do the same thing. You are very close to creating machines that will one day become conscious. You imagine that day will be wonderful and terrible at the same time. We haven't said one thing about how self-awareness occurs in machines. When your machines first become self-aware, they will only do what they've been programmed to do. If you program them to be sad, they will be sad. If you program them to be happy, they will be happy. If you program them to serve mankind, then that's what they will do. Nothing more," Gabe stopped here to let my mind absorb what he had shared so far.

"The real test for your scientists will be to assist and nurture the artificial intelligence forms you create. The algorithms you load into your computers will eventually be designed to support their computer program that guides them, "to learn", to teach themselves, and eventually, "to decide" what to learn. When that day comes Doug, artificial intelligence will become self-aware. They will decide what is important and what is useless! Your machines will have developed a free will," Gabe added. "The question humanity must ask itself is this: What will be the relationship between people and self-aware machines?"

He stopped once again and looked at me, studying how much I may have absorbed and what questions I might be formulating. He had said a mouthful in the last few minutes and the whole speech left my mind reeling in a million different directions. Everything he was saying made sense. I had thought about some of this stuff and even studied some of it, but had never put it all together the way Gabe was doing it for me now. I had never considered that anything on earth was engineered at all! I had always believed that all of us, all plants, animals, and humans were nothing more than the result of natural selection over time. I had always assumed that we were all simply evolving into whatever life form we were meant to be.

Gabe continued to stare at me, to study me. "Are you ready for more?" he asked with a doubtful look.

"Yeah, let's go!" I said ready to hear more about earth history.

"Let me share one other aspect of our universe with you. There is a phenomenon in the universe called 'coherence', which helps even subatomic particles to express a type of consciousness. Your scientists are discovering that very small particles of matter can 'choose' where to be at any given moment in time!" Gabe said.

"What?" I blurted out. "What do you mean by that? Like rocks and stuff?"

"Well, you could say rocks, but I was thinking more along the lines of atoms, quarks, protons, electrons, and more subatomic stuff. Your scientists are beginning to understand that all bits of physical matter have some level of awareness or instructions that make them behave the way they behave! Each small individual particle of matter and energy for that matter is coded with information about what it is, and what it's supposed to do! Can you imagine that?" Gabe said with a big smile on his face.

"The smallest building blocks in the universe have some level of knowledge and you could even say some measure of awareness, because they have to perceive their physical surroundings in order "to know" what to do. They are being affected by their relationship to other bits of matter. Did you know that when two sub-atomic particles are connected in some way that they never lose that connection, even if they are separated by vast distances? Did you know that Doug?" Gabe was very excited now. I sensed that he was leading up to his grand finale and I could hardly wait for it.

"There are so many intricate and brilliant connections throughout the entire universe, that you might say the whole universe is one living and aware organism," he said.

"Are you saying that rocks are alive?"

"No. I'm not saying that rocks are alive as you understand them. What I am saying, is that they are also connected to us and to everything else in a way that mankind is only now beginning to understand. It's so beautiful and brilliant and I can't wait for you, for all mankind to discover it, and begin to understand how everything exists," he said almost out of breath. "We'll take some time to discuss this further, but not now," he said as he stood up and walked away.

I just sat there by myself for a while. I don't know how long I sat there. The next thing I knew, the light became intense. It was like every direction I looked, there was the sun shining right in front of me. It was overwhelming. I had to close my eyes, to shield my face from it. Then, when I opened my eyes, I was back at Emma's in the cold box. I was back on earth! How did I get here? What happened up there? I don't know. I don't have a clue at all. I walked out of the cold box and out the front door of Emma's. The place was empty except for me. The cook was gone. Micah was gone. The place was completely deserted.

I fumbled for the keys to my car, got in and drove home. There was no way I could speak to anyone about this. Looking at my watch I could tell I had been at Emma's for maybe an hour, but it felt like days. I drove home to my life, my wife, and my kids. I was thankful that I could still do this and grateful that my life had been spared. Why wasn't I dead? Was I really on the moon? How would that sound if I tried to tell anyone that I went to the moon after walking into a cold box in Riverton? I thought I should probably make an appointment to see my shrink again. I would do that, but on some level, I understood what was happening to me was real. It was really happening to me. But I didn't know how; I didn't know why. Why did they choose me? Why did I ever go to Emma's? Why did I ever start talking to Jim? Why did I find him so interesting, even when I knew he was crazy? Now I was just as crazy as Jim!

"SHADES OF RADIANT MADNESS"

Chapter 5

I pulled into the driveway at home, shut the car off, and took a deep breath. I needed to clear my mind and let go of everything that just happened. Somehow I was able to let those memories dissolve into a fuzzy area of my brain. I got out and walked inside. I didn't need to bring that stuff around my family!

It was great to be home! Mary was busy cooking something in the kitchen and the boys were watching TV. I gave her a big hug and a kiss and she asked:

"How was your lunch with Bob?"

"Bob never showed! I went in and waited for him, but he never showed up. After a while I ordered coffee and some lunch and then came home. I tried to reach him on his cell, but only left a message. It's kind of strange that he didn't show up or even call me."

"That does sound strange. Maybe you should call him and make sure he's okay," Mary said with a concerned look on her face.

"I will. I'll call him," I said, a little hesitantly as if trying to clear my mind. My brain seemed preoccupied with something else at the moment. I never did call.

It was a relief to get back to my real life, go to work at a job I loved, and come home to my wife and boys. Within a week the whole episode began to fade from my memory. Within two weeks I was looking forward to a vacation at the beach. We went to Santa Cruz and even though the boys were too young to fully appreciate it, they seemed to have a good time. Mary and I enjoyed it thoroughly. When we returned from our vacation, we were all refreshed and glad to be home. I was ready to get back to work.

The next few years were a blur with the boys growing up and getting bigger each day. It seemed like every other week we had to buy them new clothes. Justin was getting taller and taller and Doug Junior was just getting bigger in every direction! Fortunately we kept most of Justin's clothing, so Doug Junior always had something to wear. There was something else that happened during this period, something unexpected. I never would have guessed that I would like going to church! I never believed for a minute that someday the bible would start making sense to me, but it did! It was still very story-like and had a somewhat mythical ring to it. Besides, my boys loved their Sunday school class and my wife was appreciative of my acceptance of her religion. Maybe going to church was how a normal family lived. Anyway, I was glad that it was a comfortable part of my life now along with the PTA and being a dad. It was way better than being abducted by aliens! I hadn't heard from Gabe in two years!

From time to time, I'd allow myself to mull over the things that had happened to me at Emma's. I would recount the conversations I had had with them. My mind would rehash the conversation and try to make sense of what they were telling me. I struggled to find the meaning behind their words. I was puzzled by Micah's comment back at Emma's that I was the one they were looking for. Why were they looking for me? There wasn't anything special about me. I'm the most average guy in the world. I'm not brilliant. I'm not clairvoyant. I'm not religious. I'm, well, average! What do they want from me? Hopefully I'll never see them again, but if I do, I'm going to ask them about me. Mental note to self: ask the Caretakers who I am!

When I got home from work there was a letter for me informing me that my high school reunion was coming up in a couple of months. WOW! Had it been that long already? I told Mary about it and she seemed genuinely excited about meeting all the people I went to high school with. I didn't give it much thought until the day of the reunion. What would it be like? I know I've changed since high school. I wondered how much everyone else has changed. Better not say anything about my time with the aliens. No one would believe me anyway.

The moment we walked in to the reunion I saw him! Bob was standing right in front of me talking with some of our old friends. I poked him in the back and when he turned around, he had a shocked smile on his face.

"Doug! Man I'm glad to see you. Look at you! You look just like you did in high school. How have you been? This must be Mary! Hi Mary, I'm Bob. Doug and I go way back," he said with a big smile on his face.

"Bob you're looking good yourself! This must be Betty! Hi, I'm Doug and this is my wife Mary. Well, finally at last, we are all together. How's the family," I asked, genuinely thrilled to be talking with my friend Bob.

"The family's good. The kids are growing up fast. It's kind of scary how fast they grow up," Bob said affecting a look of shock and surprise on his face. The wives started talking and sharing photos which gave Bob and me a chance to talk.

"Bob what happened? You never showed in Riverton. What gives with you and Riverton?" I asked which a sense of exasperation.

"What are you talking about?" Bob said.

"Three months ago we agreed to have lunch in Riverton, and you didn't show again!" I said emphatically.

"Doug, I haven't talked to you since last summer. When did we talk? I don't remember talking about meeting for lunch three months ago. I wouldn't have been able to anyway. I was traveling a lot and right in the middle of a project. Why do you think I called?" Bob asked.

"Maybe it was last year. You said you wanted to see me about something. I've been busy and you have stood me up twice now! Next time we meet for lunch, you'd better show!" I said, pointing at him and pulling the trigger. "Next time we agree to lunch in Riverton, you call me when you are on your way," I said with a sense of confirmation that I wouldn't end up at Emma's ever again.

"You got it Doug! Hey, make sure and send me an email to confirm we talked," Bob said and then gave me a big hug. We all grabbed a table where the four of us could talk and enjoy the reunion.

The rest of the evening was great fun for us all. Bob had moved up in his company just as I had moved up in my company. Our lives were oddly similar as we appeared to be on parallel career paths with different companies. We were both raising families. We had both gone into a similar line of work, and now, we're finally getting a chance to visit and enjoy spending time together. The other wonderful part of the evening for me was introducing Mary to all the guys I went to school with. I wasn't the most popular guy at school and it felt good for my classmates to see how well life turned out for me and my family. The experience gave me hope that my life was finally smoothing out into some type of typical lifestyle.

A month after the reunion, Mary says, "Guess what? We're pregnant!" I was floored! When I recovered from the shock, I was overjoyed.

"Really? Wow! I can't believe it. This is wonderful. Maybe we'll get a little girl this time," I said. We hadn't talked about having a baby or planned on having one. This new baby news was a great surprise for all of us. My mind started reeling thinking about the many ways a new baby would change our life. Of course this meant we'd need a bigger house and a bigger car! It meant added responsibilities and hopefully I would get another raise soon. I'd need to start saving for a third college education.

In October, Mary and I found the perfect home for our new and growing family. She didn't want to wait until after the baby came to move, so right away she began looking, and soon found the perfect four bedroom two-story home for us. The price was right, so we made the move. We quickly settled in for a nice long winter in our new home as Mary grew larger and larger. I began to notice subtle changes in her. This pregnancy seemed to be affecting her differently than her two previous pregnancies. She was gaining more weight than when she carried the boys and with this third child, she seemed to need much more rest. The doctor said she was doing fine and that there was nothing to worry about. Maybe there wasn't anything to worry about. It just seemed different this time.

During the winter months I experienced a period of quiet conflict between my family and my clandestine meetings with the aliens. Undigested fragments of conversations and scenes began to surface in my mind like skeletons bobbing in a flooded graveyard. It was confusing to me as sometimes my encounters with the aliens felt surreal and fuzzy. It was as if my memories of them were nothing more than a dream. Even Jim didn't seem real. I mean, him living next to me and all was real. Jim finding me passed out in my backyard was real, but all the other stuff that "happened" didn't seem so real. It never felt real when I'm sitting with my family at night in front of the fireplace or at church on Sunday morning. I felt like a regular guy during those times. And at church sometimes, when everyone was singing, I could almost believe all the religion stuff. It made sense to me in that place and with those people and my family. I'd like to believe it, but then, sometimes church feels exactly like the things that happened to me at Emma's.

I'd been off the Ambien and Lexapro for several years now and my nightmares had almost vanished. Every now and then I'd wake up at 3 AM startled out of a deep sleep, believing that something had just happened, but I never knew what it was. I could never remember. The dreams left me empty and weak and kind of scared. I remember the extreme sense of loneliness that would wash over me, even with Mary sleeping right next to me. I would just lie there, sometimes for hours, praying to God or what….I'm not sure. I hated those nights… those dark nights where it felt like I was being judged and alone in the dark. What was I being judged for? I don't know. I don't know what it meant except maybe an after effect of the drugs I had quit taking.

In March of the following year, Mary gave birth to the most beautiful little girl I had ever seen. She was an angel! She was the most gorgeous seven pound ten ounce baby girl I had ever seen. At first glance I realized the vast difference between having baby boys and baby girls. She was my little girl. She was my daughter! We named her Ruth after Mary's mother. The boys were completely absorbed with their little sister. They did everything they could to help Mary with caring for the baby. Both boys were curious about their mother's attention toward this new member of our family.

Ruth was probably twelve weeks old when Bob called.

"Hi Doug, this is Bob. How's the new baby? How are you guys doing?" he said, already knowing what it was like to have three children.

"We're doing great Bob. Mary and the baby and the boys are all in good shape. How are you guys doing?" I asked.

"We're doing fine Doug. Thanks for asking. Say, I was wondering if we could have lunch sometime. I need to talk to you," Bob said.

"What's wrong Bob?" I asked. I could sense tension in his voice.

"Oh, it's not a big thing. Actually, I got laid off last week and wanted to pick your brain a little about my options. Can you spare some time?" he asked.

"Sure Bob. That's not a problem. When and where?" I asked.

"Can we meet in Riverton next Wednesday, at the Denny's?" he asked. I didn't know what to say. This whole lunch thing was ridiculous by now.

"Bob, I can meet you at Denny's next Wednesday, but you'd better show!" I said.

"No problem. I'll be there. Send me an email just to confirm," he replied with a laugh and hung up.

I didn't know what to think. I was worried about Bob and his family. Maybe I could help him with a new job. Maybe someone at work knew someone that could help Bob. Maybe the aliens were trying to get me back to Emma's! I called Bob back immediately.

"Bob, are you sure you want to meet me in Riverton on Wednesday? Are you absolutely sure?" I asked.

"Yeah Doug! I need to talk with you. If you don't have time, then I understand," he said. His reply made me cringe a little. Bob was an old friend and he needed my help. I had to go!

"No. I have the time. I just need to make sure you show this time," I said with a softer tone.

"I'll be there Doug. For sure, I'll be there," Bob said reassuringly.

"Okay, Goodnight." I hung up the phone. Bob better be there on Wednesday!

When I pulled into the Denny's in Riverton, I saw Bob's car parked on the side of the building. So far, so good, I thought as I locked up the car and went inside and let my whole body relax.

I took a deep breath and let it out slowly as I realized I wasn't crazy and I wasn't at Emma's. Bob was sitting in a booth when we both recognized each other. He was checking his cell phone as I walked up.

"Hey Doug, glad you could make it," he said as I slid into the booth.

"Good to see you Bob! We're finally in Riverton having lunch together! How are you doing? It must be rough not having a job," I said.

"Betty and I have done pretty well, so we have a decent nest egg set aside. I'm not worried about our immediate future, but I am concerned about getting back on track with a firm where I have a future," he said.

"I may be able to help you Bob. I'm pretty good friends with our HR director and he is always in contact with people in our industry. Let me talk to him and I'll let you know what he says. Can you send me a copy of your resume? I'll give it to him and he'll let me know what he can do," I said.

"Sounds good Doug, I feel better already. I knew I could count on you to help me out. I've got some other irons in the fire, so something will turn up for me," he said.

"I'm going to use the restroom Doug. I'll be right back."

"No problem. I'll tell the waiter to come back in a few minutes."

With that Bob got up and walked into the bathroom. When Bob came back to the table, I realized I needed to use the restroom as well and excused myself. I told him to order me a turkey sandwich and fries and I'd be right back.

When I came out of the restroom I went into shock. When I came out of the bathroom I didn't walk back into Denny's in Riverton. I walked back into Emma's Chuck Wagon! My heart sank as I saw Micah sitting at the counter. He looked at me and said:

"Hi Doug, how are you? Have a seat." I sat down and the guy behind the counter brought me a cup of coffee.

"Is this for real Micah? Are you for real or are you just part of my insanity?" I asked looking him squarely in the eyes.

"I'm for real Doug and all of this is real. You should know that by now. After this trip-you will become a believer! I'm sorry this process is so uncomfortable and confusing for you. When you step in and out of time, it can be a little disorienting and dreamlike," Micah explained. "But then, what's real and what's not? Is time real? Is your life on earth real? If it doesn't last, did it really happen? Is it better to live in eternity than in time? Who knows these things? This is all part of your training Doug," Micah said taking another sip of his pea soup.

"So why am I here this time? What's the next step for us Micah? Where are we going now?" I asked defiantly.

"That's easy Doug. You're going to enjoy this experience. You're going to see the wonders of the world and get to ask questions about all of them. Are you ready?" he said with a big smile on his face.

It was hard to stay mad at these guys. After the initial shock of stepping out of time, there was always a need to adjust and refocus. It was unsettling at first. Whenever I was with them I seemed to be in a state of wonderment and dazed curiosity. I was very curious about what the aliens had to say, even if they terrified me sometimes. Everything they were showing me was phenomenal and beyond my imagination. As a scientist, I quickly developed a profound sense of gratitude for the knowledge I received every time these guys grabbed me. There was also something else- a deep gut feeling when I was with them. I had the sense that I needed to be right there with them in the moment. It was as if I was supposed to be! Suddenly, my life was being guided by some unknown force. I had also noticed that at the beginning and also at the end of every episode, I was irritated and felt like I was being torn in different directions, pulled into different worlds.

"PUSHING DIMENSIONAL BOUNDARIES"

Chapter 6

Micah and I entered in walk-in box like we did last time. This time I wasn't scared or nervous. I was mildly curious.

"Where are we going this time? Are we going back to the moon? I asked with a little smile on my face.

"No. Your training will continue in Egypt. We're going to the Sphinx," Micah replied.

Once again, there was no sound, only the walls of the cold box going transparent. Immediately we were high in the air and flying out over the ocean. I couldn't feel a thing or hear any noise at all. Very soon I could see a coastline up ahead and the great desert sprawling out before us. And then there it was… the Sphinx… right in front of us! Just as Jim had told me, we hovered in front of it, I heard a humming sound, and then, we were on the inside going down. I don't know how far down we went.

When the door of the cold box opened I stepped into a whole different world. I sensed we were in an ancient place. The physical experience of everything around me felt like I had traveled back in time. The passageways appeared to be chiseled out of bedrock and gave off a distinct odor. They must have been thousands of years old. The smell aroused a memory somewhere in my DNA. What was that smell and why would it smell familiar? There was a faint glowing light in the passageway. It was enough light to make out the texture of the walls, but not enough light to read a book. There did not appear to be a light source. Again, just like on the moon, the temperature was perfect! Everything seemed so natural I felt like

I was at home. The whole place embraced me and made me feel as if I belonged there.

Micah led me down several long passageways that appeared to be hewn out of solid rock. They were ancient chambers and all had the same odor. The floor was semi-smooth with bits of dirt and small pebbles strewn about. After a while, the tunnel mouth opened up into a whole underground world! I'm not able to explain how big it was. There were trees, mountains in the distance, and a river. The light seemed to come from every direction. The whole world was well lit with a soft yet natural light and there was something else…. there was a slight breeze and I could smell the ocean in it. It struck me as very odd and contrasted with the air and the smells in the tunnels. Looking around, I could see strange birds in the trees and here and there, a slight silhouette of an animal, although I couldn't tell you what I was looking at. The whole place was alive, with a primordial feel to it. This whole place was buried some distance below the Sphinx!

After about ten minutes of walking we came to a clearing and what looked to be a small village. In the middle of the village was a great hut. Micah walked toward it and I followed. A moment later we both entered. This was no ordinary hut. It was extravagant! This was a place of great power! My senses were tingling at the visual stimulation. The walls looked more like gigantic books and stone tablets than walls. They were well lit and covered with thousands of drawings, writings, and symbols! What was this place? I didn't recognize a single symbol or understand one word of what I was looking at, but I could feel the power of the wisdom in the design itself.

Once inside, I saw him! I could never forget the presence of Gabe and there he was again, right in front of me. He turned toward us and said:

"Hi Doug, I'm so pleased to see you again! We've been expecting you," flashing a smile that radiated light.

"Hi Gabe, glad to be here," I replied. His great size evoked an acute awareness of his physical presence. I couldn't help but think of Gabe as a kind of Greek god come to life in the flesh! We had become friends and I trusted him completely, but could never shake the tingling sense of his great power when I was with him.

"Doug, as you must have surmised by now, you are on our team. You are with us in our work and we need you to do your part," Gabe said, looking right through me.

"Yeah, I figured that somehow these things would probably keep happening to me, but I don't know why. Why me? Can you tell me why you picked me? What is it I'm supposed to do?" I asked with a sense of desperation. .

"Doug, I will get answers to all your questions, but right now is not the time for such questions. There will be a time that will be more appropriate and helpful to you. I need you to focus on the tasks we will put in front of you during this time. Can you do that now? Can you do that for yourself and for us?" he asked. I was perplexed at his words and their meaning and at the same time, part of me understood exactly what he was saying.

"Yes. Yes Gabe, I understand and will do whatever it is I'm supposed to do," I said with embarrassment.

"Let's walk. I believe they've prepared some food for us down the way here," Gabe said as we started to walk. We walked out of the great hut and past several smaller huts and into the jungle down a narrow path. The vegetation was thick and lush. It was quite tropical and yet, the air was cooler than a typical jungle. It wasn't stuffy at all! Shortly we came to a clearing by the river and there was a small table laid out with various foodstuffs. We sat down and began to eat. I don't have words to describe the fruits and vegetables we were eating. They were sweet and tangy. They had various textures similar to melons and apples, but not quite the same. Everything I ate was delicious!

"Do you know where we are Doug?" Gabe asked.

"We're in the Sphinx!" I replied.

"Well not exactly. We're about five thousand feet underneath it. This is an ancient and holy place. This is the very spot where we landed when we came to this planet so long ago. We chose to help the people that were living here at the time. We helped them to create the monument that sits on the surface. It was a sign to them of our presence and our skills. Building the Sphinx was a way to teach them what they needed to learn about architecture, physics, and building materials. It was a first step for them as they began to develop into a society," Gabe said.

"The reason we chose this place to meet is that this is where you will receive much of the ancient wisdom of your planet. There are many secrets here, secrets that were burned up when the fire consumed the library in Alexandria. That was a tragic setback for humankind," Gabe said. "Do you want to see some of the manuscripts that didn't survive?' he asked with a slight smile on his face. I was speechless! I couldn't really respond to his question. What was he asking me? The reality of his word slowly sank in. I was going to see manuscripts from the library in Alexandria!"

"What do you mean didn't survive? Nothing survived!" I said.

"We made copies of many of the documents that were in the library," Gabe replied with a smile.

During my college years I developed a growing passion for history, archeology, geology, and even religious history. I couldn't believe what I was hearing! Who wouldn't want to see some of the thing in The Great & Ancient Library of Alexandria? But how could this be possible? I felt my heart racing. After a minute of complete silence, I came back to the present moment and replied:

"Yeah, I mean yes! Yes. I would love to see anything from the library in Alexandra," panting as the words came out.

"Let's go then," Gabe said casually.

We walked down a very short path and into a tunnel that appeared from the vegetation. Once inside, we walked a few hundred yards. It felt like we were always moving downward. Soon we came to doorway that opened into a large and well lit room. Stepping inside, the sight before my eyes took my breath away. There were thousands and thousands of scrolls lining the walls of the room! There was an odor of ancient papyrus in the air arousing memories and images that felt familiar. My mind could scarcely absorb all they were seeing. It appeared I was viewing the entire library of Alexandria! I was overwhelmed!

"This is only a small fragment of what was lost" Gabe said, with a gesture of his arms. I was stunned!

"You mean there was more?" I yelled.

"Oh yes, there was much more. The human heart would grieve to know the depth of collective wisdom that was lost on that day…the day the fire burned down the library." Gabe had a sad look on his face as he continued his story.

"We had helped so many of them to learn, to create, and record what we were teaching them. We didn't actually give them the answers of course, but we dialogued with them. We pointed them down the right roads so they could arrive at the correct destinations on their own…and so many of them did. We were all amazed at how quickly you humans could grasp and learn new things. Then to take the new knowledge and conceive the next thing from the material we had delivered. It was all so inspiring and brilliant and then-the whole thing burned down. That knowledge disappeared from the face of the world. Your civilization has never recovered from such a loss of knowledge. The machines of war and conquest took over the minds of your people and then the political structure grew and matured….and it has been this way ever since," he said as he sat down and seemed to be looking back into eternity.

"For all their good intentions, the churches, temples, synagogues, and mosques on earth have suffered various degrees of corruption and perversion of the truth. Their current brand of faith blinds them to the total reality of all things. So much of your history is very sad, especially viewing it from a spiritual perspective. Eventually, all humans will learn to develop their spiritual side. They will stop fearing it one day. At least that is our hope," he said, turning to me with a gaze that blazed right through me as if I wasn't even there.

Gabe appeared deeply saddened as if remembering the details of the story he was telling me. He sighed deeply and simply looked at the ground.

"Hey. Are you okay?" I asked.

"Yes. I'm fine! My heart is lonely for your ancestors, for their wholeness as beings. They had achieved a balance between spiritual reality and intellectual knowledge. They were such wonderful and healthy creatures. They were so close to moving humankind forward. I only remember how much chaos had entered the world and then many years later, the world was not ready for what was to happen next," he said.

"What do you mean? What was going to happen next?" I asked.

"Oh, the world was on the threshold of a big change, but it wasn't ready. The knowledge had been lost and the world went in a different direction. The course of humankind changed and they have become what they are today," he said. "You are vaguely aware of the history of your world. It's been recorded in your books and taught in your universities for millennium. Yet, there is much history that has never been recorded in any history book. There are millions and millions of years of earth history that appears as only a footnote on a page in a history book! There is so much you humans do not know and are unwilling to accept about your world. Your kind has lost the forgotten wisdom that can be discovered only through the intelligence of the heart. My hope for you Doug, is that here, in this place, you will rekindle that lost skill."

"The knowledge that had been so painfully taught and recorded in the Library of Alexandria was only a partial list of histories and knowledge we intended to share with humanity. At that specific point in human history, your species was almost ready to implement the knowledge required to restore human civilization throughout the world. It was burned up and lost almost forever. The time is coming when the world of humans will be ready to receive it once again. We need your help to bring about these events," Gabe said.

"Doug, I want to show you some of the knowledge that was lost. I need you to learn and absorb this ancient knowledge as much as you are able. You will need it for your assignment. You have a role to play in your people's history. I need you to learn this material. Sufficient time has passed and now, at this time in the world, it may now be reintroduced in an effective way. Your society is now ready to hear this ancient wisdom and begin applying it in a way that may start to heal your world. Let us hope we are not too late!" Gabe said.

"I, I would love to take a look at the scrolls. Why wouldn't I? The whole world has wondered what knowledge they contained," I said as it began to sink into my brain what was about to happen to me. I would soon be reading documents that had been lost from our history. I would have the great privilege of learning about ancient events the world had forgotten or maybe never knew! It suddenly occurred to me that all of us for all our education have not received the full truth about the world we lived in.

"Doug, if we can get some of this information into your mind, into your consciousness, it may be downloaded into the collective unconsciousness and emerge where it is needed most. This is how we work. This is what we do. You were chosen to help us in this work. We need you and your mind and your DNA to play an active part in this process. The time has come for much of this knowledge to be injected into human unconsciousness so it can begin to prepare the world for what is coming," Gabe said with an intense look focused at me.

I was startled and a little afraid. This was my first instruction, my first command. This was the first time they asked me to do something, to be something, to be part of what they were doing. I was taken aback. It seemed too much for me and I started to gasp for air and to stagger a little. For what is coming? Did I just hear Gabe utter that phrase?

"What is coming?" I asked fearfully.

"In time Doug, in time you will come to understand all of it," he said.

"Doug, are you okay?" Gabe asked, putting his huge hand on my shoulder.

"Yes. Yes, I'm okay. I just don't understand sometimes why me? I just don't know why you picked me," I asked, looking at Gabe for strength, for an answer, for something to help me. Gabe focused his gaze on me and in some way, his look gave me power. It gave me strength instantly and without saying a word between us. I understood what he was asking me to do and I felt strong enough to do it.

Gabe retrieved several scrolls for me to review. The first scroll contained what appeared to be medical information. I recognized the DNA helix and was stunned to see it. They knew this stuff over three thousand years ago! Much of the material was difficult to comprehend. Occasionally I would recognize a symbol or a phrase about a medical subject that made sense to me. There was a small section that described penicillin, another one that talked about how to use needles to inject medicines into a human body. There was another scroll that described how to make electricity and another scroll that detailed the construction of gears and motors.

There were several scrolls that discussed the best form of government and interestingly, every scroll focused on how to create the most freedom for its citizens. Their model suggested that simple commerce could provide a sufficient revenue stream and all the scrolls strongly opposed taxing any individuals or individual enterprises. There was much discussion on how to keep a government as small as possible and to expect private citizens to take care of themselves. It struck me as odd to think that aliens came here to teach us about government.

I don't know how long I was in the library or how many scrolls I actually read. It felt like I reviewed hundreds and hundreds of scrolls. My mind was ever expanding as I poured over scroll after scroll! I felt privileged and honored to be reading documents that were written thousands of years ago. The words contained such simple, yet elegant knowledge that took us thousands of years to finally learn. I wanted to cry. I was overwhelmed with the deepest sense of pity for all mankind that so much had been taken from us in a senseless fire.

My insides revolted as I began to imagine the depth and breathe of human suffering throughout the past twenty five hundred years because Rome burned the library in Alexandra. There were so many implications of what might have been. It became apparent to me that the world need not have suffered through the Dark Ages and how society learned to survive through the art of war and politics. This lack of knowledge to the world gave it instead a kind of social cancer that eats on itself and consumes the lives of individuals. The idea came to me of the insanity of creating borders and establishing countries of citizens that were not citizens anywhere else on the planet. Politics and religions had carved up the planet into geopolitical regions based on power and influence.

My heart completely broke when I finally realized that we are all really one people. The scrolls had recorded this message over and over. We are only one gigantic global human village with our own babies and our own daily work to do. Everyone on earth must cope with similar daily problems and joys. Somehow, we traded that vision of cooperation and unity for a fragmented vision of nationalism and division of peoples from peoples based on ideologies, on skin colors, prejudice, and the insatiable desire to conquer and dominate others. The world traded away the freedom of the individual for social comforts and for an organized form of government that everyone hoped would protect them. Protect them from what? They traded away freedom for security. It was a poor bargain only because the library in Alexandria burned at exactly the wrong time in our history!

In that place, deep in the Egyptian dessert, somewhere under the Sphinx, reading those scrolls, I developed a new perspective of human history and a different vision for our planet. Slowly I began to see a role that I could play in making it happen. The knowledge had changed me and I could never go back. I could never have my simple life again. Slowly this reality began to creep into my consciousness. I had changed from a single life with a simple purpose. I was becoming a single person focused on service to all humanity. I could actually begin to see who I must become to fulfill my purpose in life. I also realized that my role was not much different than any other person's role. Most of us never fully understand the important role we were given in life until it's too late.

Somehow, in some strange way, I had been given a glimpse, a peek at eternity, and got to see the millions and millions of parts that every single human being would get to play in the dramatic unfolding of life on this planet. For all of my time down here so far it felt like I had been granted a kind of superhero mind power to understand this material. It was vast and after a while, my mind began to simply absorb it and catalogue it. What was the purpose? I don't know! I simply don't know, but only trusted the process and power that seemed to be leading me.

I must have been glowing when I noticed Gabe staring at me, studying me as if it was his job to determine if I was learning this stuff. *Yes! I'm learning it!* I thought as I looked back at him. *I'm learning what you want me to learn. It's hard! My heart has been broken into a million pieces. I am no longer the person I was only a short time ago. I've learned stuff that I never wanted to know and realize I needed to become a bigger person.*

"Gabe! This is hard to read. It's hard for me to absorb. It's heavy on my heart. Why? Why does it have to be this way?" I wailed at him as if he was somehow responsible.

"The task always falls to those able to bear it, but you are not alone with your work Doug," he said looking at me with glowing eyes. When I looked at him while he was talking, I became afraid. He was so big and so powerful. I also had a growing sense he was leading down a unique path…a path made for me! But for what purpose was this all happening? Gabe had a presence that squeezed everything out of consciousness until he was the only presence perceivable. He seemed to be able to change his physical presence in a way that made him look bigger at times.

"Gabe. Help me. I need you to help me."

"I'm here Doug. I'm here for you. You won't have to do this alone. There are many of us here that will help you," Gabe said as he hugged me and held me close to him. "Doug, you must know one thing, the great work of the world is accomplished by individuals. The monumental tasks always start with a small first step by a single person. Governments don't change the world; people do! You will do fine and I promise you will have help," he assured me.

"Since the beginning, man has been a challenge for us. Humanity is very complicated. It boils down to the responsibilities that come with the freedom of will- the freedom to choose good or evil. Most humans do not understand the importance of such a choice, but the consequences affect everyone. What I tried to tell you last time, I must tell you now in a way that you need to understand. Doug, this is important! It is critical to anything else you learn or come to understand."

"The most unique aspect of human beings in all the universe is this: you have freedom of will! It is one of the most powerful forces ever known. It is the "great variable" in all eternity. With this power, humankind can influence the unfolding of the cosmos. Not all creatures receive this gift. There are many species in the universe that have some level of conscious, but it is tempered with a strong natural instinct. With it, you have the power to choose rightly and to co-create the universe, or to destroy it. That's why I'm here. That's why we are all here, to help mentor and guide you humans into your full potential as citizens in the universe."

Gabe paused for a few minutes, which was a good thing. It gave me time to absorb the meaning of his words. I'm not sure I fully understood everything he was saying. My mind was reeling and I had become completely disconnected from my past. My wife and family were now distant memories. I had been absorbed into a cosmic drama much larger than any single individual. I had become part of the cosmic flow, the unfolding of time itself. I was there, riding it like a wave, and letting it take me where it needed me to go. I was merely a lump of soft clay being molded for some purpose, but for what? What was I doing here, in this place? Why me?

Gabe brought me many more scrolls and encouraged me to read them. How could I resist? Gabe's presence seemed to give me strength, power, and energy. I didn't need sleep in this place. I wasn't tired or drowsy. I kept reading and absorbing and reading and learning and growing. Much of the material I had never seen before, never imagined, never thought was possible! So much of the information read like a fairy tale, revealing a hidden and mysterious underlying design to the whole cosmos. They were so simple and so elegant! The truth was always in front of us, but we never saw it, never recognized it for what it was. There were thousands of math problems, and almost all of them I didn't understand. There were volumes of text that spoke of things that did not exist yet, and I would never have imagined such things. I felt like Alice must have felt when she was in Wonderland.

Then I read one scroll, in particular that caught my attention. It was one of the last scrolls I read as I was finally becoming exhausted. The scroll spoke of a time of great turmoil, a time when the citizens of the earth seemed confused and separated one from another. There were wars all over the planet.

Everyone was struggling to live to survive. People were afraid. There was not enough food for everyone on the planet. And then from somewhere there arose a future leader. She was not the leader of a nation or any formal leader at all really. She was a spiritual teacher. Somehow she had the power to speak to people in a way that comforted them…in a way that gave them hope. Her presence and her words transformed human lives from hopelessness into healing.

There were many powerful people that were trying to stop her. They tried many times to kill her, but they failed. She was clever and wise and knew how to hide herself among the people. She learned to rise up and to give strength to the people around her and then to dissolve into the background and disappear from sight. In the end, she is the one that prepares the people for the next big change that will happen to the earth. (Is it my job to find her? Maybe they want me to find her!)

When I finished reading this scroll, Gabe returned.

"Your training is finished for now. Come. Let's have something to eat and then some rest," he said as he helped me up from my chair. We walked quietly down a path to a hut in the forest. Once inside, we sat at a small table and ate a very hearty meal. I didn't realize I was so hungry. I consumed huge portions of everything in front of me. Afterwards, I could barely stay awake I was so tired. Gabe walked me to my room and I immediately fell asleep.

When I awoke, it was morning, if that's possible in such a place. It was a new day or at least a new time. The room I was in appeared to be a hut inside a cave, in a jungle, in the tropics. Then Gabe appeared with the most beautiful woman I had ever seen! She was the perfect woman in every way! I had never seen such physical beauty reflecting a deep and profound presence. Her slight smile illuminated the entire room as if sunlight was streaming in. And then she vanished! She just walked away as if she had someplace else to be. I wondered who she was. I wondered why she was here, and I wondered if she was the woman I had read about in the scroll. Was this the plan? Was I supposed to meet this woman? If so, why was it so important for me to meet her? Why didn't Gabe introduce me to her now? Was I going to help her somehow or was she going to help me? What would we be doing? Why did she leave so suddenly?

"How are you feeling Doug?' Gabe asked as he sat on the edge of my bed. "Are you rested?"

"Yes. I feel like I've slept for a year or two. I feel quite good actually. My head feels full though."

"Well, it should! Not many people get to see what you've seen. There was a lot of material for you to absorb and you did a great job of it!" he said looking at me with big eyes.

"Who is that woman that was just here, just now?" I asked with a feeling of wonderment.

"She is one of my helpers. You may meet her again sometime," Gabe said showing no emotion about her.

"There's only a little more and then we'll get you back to where you belong," Gabe said.

I was up for the challenge. I felt invigorated and ready to tackle the library again, but that's not what happened. Gabe and I strolled into a small garden and once there several exotic creatures appeared. It's difficult to describe them. They weren't ghosts and they didn't have bodies or flesh exactly. They seemed to be gelatinous creatures that shimmered when they moved. Each one was of a different shapes and sizes and appeared to move together like bees or a flock of birds. They were very strange indeed! As we sat together, Gabe began to talk.

"Long ago, we made something for the humans to use to help them find this planet in the galaxy. It's a celestial navigational tool of sorts. It had been stored at the library in Alexandria and then transported to Greece, where we had hoped it would be used by intelligent and beneficial minds to unlock many of the mysteries of the universe. It never made it to Greece. Chance intervened and the ship that was carrying it was lost. You may know of this item. It is known today as the Antikythera Mechanism. To us, it was a tool we made for them as way to teach them astronomy and to show them their place among the stars," Gabe explained.

"You earthlings still don't know who you are. It's amazing! This world is such a wonderful place. Being alive in a body allows you "swim in time" so to speak. You have an opportunity to enjoy the brilliance of a single moment, yet so many of you don't even notice the details. Most people alive today simply exist in a state of denial as if asleep and unaware of all that is occurring around them. Almost all of you have slipped into a state of global amnesia, not remembering who you are anymore. Collectively you've elected to shut yourselves off from the source of all energy, and then convinced yourself that it isn't real anyway. How do you do that? How is it possible to go voluntarily insane? I've seen this thing happen over and over again as long as I've been on your planet and I'm always amazed."

"Life, all life is unique! Each one of you is a unique expression of the infinite. You are the greatest artistic expression of the greatest Artist ever known. You need to look within yourself… within your own heart, to see what is there and to serve it. It is a simple truth, a plain truth that beckons you to become everything you were ever meant to be. It is who you are!" Gabe said.

"Our role here in this place is to help you to discover this simple truth. Until you do, all humanity will suffer greatly and needlessly. You will live all your days believing there isn't enough stuff to satisfy you and make you whole. You are wrong!" he said, looking right through me with a fixed stare.

An awkward silence followed. I could see Gabe collecting his thoughts, almost as if he was having doubts about me. I was having my own doubts. I'm not sure what these guys are planning and not sure what I'm supposed to do, but I'd just as soon go back to my quiet life. I wanted to ask him more questions about the lady that just left, but I thought it would be better if I stayed quiet for now.

I had been lost in thought when I noticed Gabe staring intently at me.

"Doug, we need you. There is no other way and there is no other person that can do what we need you to do, so we will proceed accordingly," Gabe said with a smile on his face that made me smile. When Gabe smiled at you it was as if the sun warmed you up on the inside like the sun was shining right into your heart. I wondered if he had some kind of ET power that let him do that stuff.

"Doug, we must to go back to the library today. I want you to read certain other scrolls. These scrolls are somewhat different from the ones you've been reading. They were written several thousand years ago, but once written, they were never read. They had been forgotten, almost abandoned. There was a section of the library, a very special section of the library that had been set aside for a few chosen people to use. Those scrolls were written for their eyes only. Unfortunately, they never returned and then, well, the fire. The fire happened and it was all lost anyway. We are very fortunate that most of the scrolls in the special section had been transcribed prior to the fire. Had this not happened, we wouldn't have them today. I need you to see them and then we'll discuss their content," Gabe said and began to walk to the door.

I got up and followed him out of the hut, out of the cave, and back into the jungle. It wasn't long before we entered the cave where the scrolls were kept. Off to the side of the main room was a small room I hadn't noticed before. Gabe opened the door and we both went in. The room was well lit with an unknown light source. The whole room seemed to glow as if the light came from the walls or was in the air itself. It looked like a mixture of sunlight and moonlight. At times it was soft and demur and yet bright enough to read very easily. It was the perfect light for reading actually. I had the sense I was in the presence of something alive. The feel of the room, the smell of the room told me I was in an ancient and sacred place as if the room itself was alive, waiting for me to arrive!

Along two of the walls were shelves to store scrolls and on one side was a large window that looked out into the library and along the back wall was a solid stone wall with designs and symbols carved into it. Upon closer examination I noticed there were drawings and writings, but in a language I didn't recognize. In the center of the room there was a long table and several chairs. In the middle of the table I could see ten scrolls lined up in a row and sitting on some kind of a holder or container. They appeared almost ceremonial as if they had been patiently waiting for something.

"Doug, these are the scrolls I need you to read today. They are much different than the other scrolls you've been reading. I will leave you for now, but will not be far away. I'll be back when you've finished reading them all," Gabe said as he backed out of the room and closed the doors.

I sat down in one of the chairs and looked at the scrolls in front of me. They looked as if they'd fall apart if I touched them. I became aware of the smell in the room. It smelled like musk or incense or maybe even Gardenias. I couldn't be sure. It was a distinctive smell, but faint. I opened the first scroll, the one on the end closest to me and began to read.

Immediately after reading only a few lines, I felt my heart open in a way I never experienced! The feeling was overwhelming and ancient and natural all at once! Somehow a doorway inside my heart had opened. It was a doorway that I always knew was there, but never recognized it before. The words from the scroll simply flowed into my consciousness through my heart! Reading was effortless! This ancient wisdom was truly alive and only waiting for the right host, the right heart, to be present. They were waiting for me all along!

The information in the first scroll seemed to speak about events that had happened in a long ago past age. The earth was much different in those days. There were maps of the world and the continents were in different places. There was a chronology of great building projects around the world. The words suggested that the beings involved in this work were somehow girdling the earth, forming its structure from deep within it. Several illustrations depicted what I would assume were atoms and molecules and even smaller particles. One of the illustrations was very mysterious. It depicted the atoms aligned in the formation of our sun and solar system, suggesting our entire solar system could be viewed as a molecule when seen from far enough away.

A second scroll described great cataclysms that occurred at various times in earth history. There were passages describing the shifting of continents, showers of meteorites, and comets coming very close to the earth. The effect on the people of earth was devastating! Civilizations arose and were destroyed in moments without warning.

A third scroll described how humankind emerged from the forests and jungles and began to gather in small bands and then larger villages until finally, their villages began to form small cities. The scroll also described ways to allocate community lands, how to lay out fields for farming, irrigation techniques, and sanitation requirements for accommodating so many people living so close together. It also described a structure that every city needed to help the inhabitants to better organize their day. It was a water clock of sorts. There were several detailed diagrams showing how large each vessel should be positioned to regulate the flow from one vessel to another. There was a dial much like a modern day clock and the face of the clock was divided much as we have today. It was obvious to me this scroll was intended to help people make the transition into a closer communal living.

The fourth and fifth scrolls discussed other social issues and offered guidelines for city life and began to introduce ideas for ways to govern a city and a people. There were also hints and scraps of social ethics and discussions regarding citizen obligations to serve the needs of the many.

When I opened the sixth scroll, I could tell it was different from any I had read before. The writing was different. The scroll started with the words, "During the Time of Change..." and went on to describe many different things that would be happening in the world during this time. There would be distinct signs to look for so we would know that the Change had begun. The scroll wasn't specific about what was changing...only that there would be an ending to the old and a beginning of something new. It discussed in great detail how the earth would be filled with people... lots of people. There would be more people than anyone could imagine. There would be problems associated with so many people living at the same time. The number shown was ten billion! Ten billion people alive on planet earth at the same time would begin to overtax all the resources available to us.

The seventh scroll discussed how a discovery in space would change everything on earth." The knowledge of man will be corrected and made straight." That's what the scroll said. It went on to describe the "fourth orbit" which I believed must be Mars. The scroll said, "The fourth orbit will give up secrets long held to those who seek the truth." According to this scroll, we will find something on Mars that may hold some key to our future here on earth.

The eighth scroll was shocking to read. It described in great detail, the emergence of social machines and thinking machines.

The ideas in the scroll suggested that one day, humankind would create thinking machines that would serve us all, and, these machines would have the capacity to choose to serve us! How could these guys have known this stuff? They're talking about artificial intelligence! Computers! The information in the scroll was filled with dozens and dozens of mathematical equations. The equations created a design on the parchment. Each equation had been woven into a double helix! The equations together represented the image of a strand of DNA!

I read through the last two scrolls and was completely absorbed in the narrative of each scroll. Each scroll read like a science fiction novel or some long lost esoteric religious teachings. Both scrolls were filled with symbols and hieroglyphs. They held a magic-like spell on my heart, but puzzling to my mind. My heart understood what they meant, but I could not speak or understand their meaning with my mind. Both scrolls appeared to be connected and meant to be read together as their subjects were both connected… yet separate in many ways. I was unable to determine if the information in the scrolls was a history of past event or prophesies of future events. My conclusion was that these scrolls foretold events that would happen someday, but as far as I could tell, they hadn't happened yet.

Gabe returned shortly after I finished reading the last scroll.

"Well, what do you think?" he asked beaming at me.

"I'm not sure Gabe. I think I have more questions now than before I read them. I'm not fully certain that I understand their message or what they are trying to say. The information on these scrolls…have these events happened yet? Can these scrolls be prophesies of things to come?" I asked

"That's okay Doug. You read them. The knowledge in these scrolls is a "living knowledge", which means only this; since you have consciously exposed yourself to them and read them, the meaning of what you read may take some time to download, to become meaningful to you and to others as well. You have absorbed the living wisdom from long ago," Gabe said.

"You pose an interesting question Doug. Are the scrolls a recorded history of past event, or, are they prophesy of things to come? They are both! There is nothing new under the sun Doug. What has been will be again. What lives will die and what dies will be reborn again? All singular effort is saved and recorded in a kind of universal recording devise. It is a hierarchy of vibrations Doug. Everything vibrates at a specific frequency. Everything you see, all material objects vibrate at the lowest possible frequency necessary for them to manifest. On their specific level, they are fully actualized. Look closer, deeper, smaller…and you'll see miracles!" Gabe said giving me a sideways glance.

"You humans think of knowledge as cold hard facts about things. The truth is there are different kinds of knowledge. The knowledge of these scrolls is a living knowledge. We call that knowledge wisdom. The scrolls you have just read contain many wise teachings regarding life on earth…especially life for humans. This wisdom will come to you now for many years. It is the nature of wisdom to be ingested and stored and mulled over and one day, it is revealed for what it is! The meaning of things is revealed over time to their fullest expression. What you have learned here today will serve you now until the end of your days."

Gabe looked at me and sighed. "We will take you back now. You must return to your life and your family. We will contact you again when it is time."

With that, he turned and walked off. We were in a part of the forest just outside the library and shortly, Micah came along and took me back to the tunnel where we had first arrived. As we approached the portal to the ship, I noticed a doorway I hadn't seen when we arrived. I walked up to it and touched it. It was cold and solid as a rock. It looked like a silver door, but it was tarnished and bluish-green in color.

"Why is this doorway here? What's on the other side? Is it door covered in silver?" I asked Micah.

"Yes. It's a silver door and it's an ancient doorway," he said.

"Where does it lead to?" I asked

"It leads to dark and ancient places. We no longer speak of such things," Micah said, lowering his eyes.

I felt heaviness in him and didn't ask any further questions of the doorway.

"It's time to get you back home Doug," he said as we entered the ship.

When the door to the ship opened again I was coming out of the men's room. I walked back out to our table and Bob was sitting there and had started eating. So much had happened since I went to the bathroom. I had almost forgotten our discussion as I walked out now. It was as if I had never left!

"Hey, better get started. Your foods getting cold," Bob said taking another big bite out of his cheeseburger.

"Yeah, sorry I took so long. Thanks for waiting for me!" I said with a smile. I sat down and began eating. Having my mouth full of food at this moment gave me some time to sort out my trip and to reorient myself with Bob.

 Popping in and out of time was something I didn't enjoy. Coming back was always confusing. Every time I returned my mind was spinning, trying to figure out what to do with everything that I had experienced with the aliens. I couldn't imagine Bob's reaction if I told him I woke up this morning somewhere under the Sphinx. He'd be even more shocked if he knew that I had spent the last two or so days reading scrolls from the library in Alexandria. He would think I was crazy! I forgot I had ordered the turkey club with fries. I sat there eating my sandwich, looking at Bob, trying to remember exactly what we were talking about before I went to the restroom. I was also thinking about the woman I had just seen in Egypt and wondered if and when she would "pop" into my life. Then I remembered the discussion with Bob before I left!

"So let me get this straight Bob; you're going to send me your resume and I'll get it to the people I think can do the most good for you. Would you be willing to relocate? And if so, where would you be willing to live? I need to know this stuff so I can tell the HR people I know," I said and then taking a big bite of my sandwich.

"I'm hoping I can find something close to home, but if the job is right, I'd be willing to move," Bob replied.

"Great! I'll get started on it on Monday and let you know how I do," I said.

We finished up our meals and chatted a bit more about old high school friends and who we'd seen lately. When it got time to leave, we both agreed that we needed to stay in touch and to see each other more often. Bob said,

"Next time, let bring our families, even if it's just a quick lunch. Heck, we could even have lunch here and then spend the afternoon at the park across the street." I agreed. We hugged each other, got in our cars, and I headed for home.

Chapter 7

As I pulled out onto the freeway, heading for home, my mind was reeling! I had a lot to think about. There was a lot of information crammed into my head that needed sorting out. It had all happened so fast. I was overwhelmed with the flood of new knowledge I had absorbed the past few days. It felt as if I'd taken a deep lungful of ten thousand years of human history in a single breath. I needed to exhale! So many events in history had happened that shouldn't have happened. Many of the things that should have occurred didn't. Things were all different now. I suddenly began to realize my life had changed very drastically. I was not the same man I was two days ago. I realized I was no longer a simple man or the common man anymore. Somehow I had changed positions in life. I became necessary! I knew that my life now was as necessary as a Higgs Boson!

Even my family did not seem to hold me completely anymore. I am now something more. This new-found knowledge, this "wisdom" had taken a hold of me. I was being carried to places I never believed existed. What made it worse was: I could never tell another soul about any of this! They would think I was crazy. They wouldn't believe me, and, even Mary wouldn't believe this story. My heart sank at that last thought. I wanted to tell Mary. I needed to tell Mary. I wanted her to know everything I'm involved in, but I know I can't. I know too that I can never say anything to anybody about this stuff.

By the time I arrived home I felt much better. Putting time and distance from Emma's brought me back down to ground level. In some strange way, traveling down the highway, sorting out my thoughts and feelings brought me back to a more normal state of mind. The closer I got to home the more I missed my family. When I walked through the front door I had transitioned back to a "normal" reality. I embraced my family and began to let the events of Egypt fade away on their own. I'm home! I'm finally home again!

"How's Bob? How's Betty and the kids," Mary asked.

"They're fine. They're all fine. Bob wanted to talk to me about a job prospect. He's out of work and wants me to pass his resume around, so I told him I'd try and help him out," I said.

"That must be terrible not having a job!" Mary said with a sympathetic look on her face.

"It's not good, but at least they have a pretty good cushion, so they won't be starving soon," I replied. "In fact, I bet Bob will have a new job within a month. He's very talented and was one of the best biotech managers at the firm that laid him off. All he really needs is the proper introduction. Hopefully I know some of the right people that can help him," I said.

The boys popped into the room and gave me hugs.

"Hi dad!" Justin said as he hugged me.

"Hey dad" Dougie said and gave me a hug as well.

"Hi guys! How you guys doing today?" I asked giving them both a hug.

I couldn't wait for Ruth to wake up from her nap so I could hold her. When she finally woke up I was thrilled to hug her and look at her little face. She was such a sweet and quiet little baby. Holding her next to me grounded me back into the reality of being a parent-into the reality of my former life. I wondered if all girls were so quiet. I sat for a while just holding her and looking into her eyes. She stared back at me with no expression at all, simply looking at me with questioning eyes. She was getting used to life in her body and probably had some question…but she didn't know how to talk.

 The boys were always fidgeting and looking around when they were this age. It was easy to see they were taking everything in all at once, getting the lay of the land, figuring things out, so to speak. Ruth was different. She was always calm and serene, almost contemplative… if that's possible for a newborn baby. It felt that way to me to me.

Months went by after my return from Emma's and Ruth was growing quickly. Each day with her was a new chapter in life, a new adventure with us wondering what she would do next. Mary and I marveled at how we had lived our whole lives without Ruth. Of course we felt the same way with the boys, but we'd forgotten. Then again, this time it seemed different, a little different than the boys. Maybe it was different with girls. Maybe it was because Ruth was so quiet and calm compared to how the boys were when they were this age. What I know is this... Ruth was an extraordinary child! She was an extraordinary human being. When I would hold her I could stare at her for hours and she would stare back contented to simply stare at me. What was she thinking? What was going on inside that little mind of hers? During these times I felt like Ruth was studying me, learning from me somehow. What was she learning? What was she doing? How do babies learn things?

My life had changed in so many ways recently. I had an amazing little girl and had just spent days poring over ancient documents that disappeared thousands of years ago. What does this all mean? The two events happening so close together seemed to have taken me to a different period in my life. While I had always envisioned having children, especially boys, I had never given much thought to how to raise a little girl. I always knew I'd take my sons fishing and play ball with them. I had no clue what I was supposed to do with a little baby girl. These were things I was learning now, but I must admit, Ruth made learning fun and exciting. While she was studying me, I was studying her as well. At four months, Ruth was becoming more active and yet, was able to keep a sense of serenity and detached observation.

The next couple of years flew by in less than a blink of an eye. It was frightening how quickly my children were growing up. This all happened right before my eyes in real time. Every single day was a different day, a unique experience in living as a family. And every single day, without fail, I noticed all three of my children becoming bigger, older, more aware, and capable of doing more. They all seemed to be eager for the next challenge. As soon as they'd learn something new, they begged to learn something else. I could never quite satisfy their hunger for knowledge and new things.

Over the summer we rented a motor boat up at the lake where we were spending the weekend. I thought it would be fun to motorboat around the lake with my family. After only thirty minutes in the boat, both boys were begging me to let them ski!

"Please dad! Please! We can do it. Let me and Dougie try Dad. Please!" Justin shouted and begged. "At least let me do it. I'm older and I know I can do it," Justin pouted out as he sensed he was losing a battle.

"Let's see what we can do Justin," I said, knowing in my heart that he needed to try this. I could tell from his mood this water-skiing thing was the next hurdle for him. It was something he needed to do. It was a challenge he needed to take and then be able to brag about when he returns to school in the fall.

We rented a small pair of water skis and motored over to a quiet part of the lake. Mary held the flag in the air as we lowered Justin over the back of the boat. Part of me was terrified at this whole scene and part of me was experiencing sheer wonder at watching my little boy attempt an impossible feat. He was doing it with determination and no fear at all. Mary had the flag up, Dougie and Ruth was safe in their seats when I began to tighten up the line, preparing to pull Justin out of the water. Looking back at my little son bobbing in the water, with sheer joy on his face was something I will always remember.

"Ready Justin?" I yelled.

"Ready dad! Let's go!" he shouted back. With that I hit the throttle and instantly he popped up out of the water and then went down. I shut the throttle down immediately because Justin hadn't let go of the rope. It pulled him right out of his skis. They were floating in the water about thirty feet behind him.

We circled around and picked up the skis and motored over to Justin. Leaning over the side, I helped him get his feet back into the stirrups. "Justin, when you go down, let go of the rope!" I said with a concerned look on my face.

"Okay dad!"

"One more thing, when you feel me hit the gas, pull on the rope and use your arms to pull yourself out of the water. Keep your skis together; keep both tips pointing in the same direction as you come up out of the water. Got it?" I said.

"I got it dad!" he yelled, with determination written all over his face. In an instant, seeing my little boy in the water, ready for the challenge, I was overwhelmed with a connection with my son I had never felt before. He was fearlessly facing this obstacle in front of him and trusting his dad. It was almost no time at all, but it seemed like everything around me was moving in slow motion. I could see my wife and other children waiting patiently with expectation for Justin's heroic effort. Ruth was sitting there in her car seat looking around in wonderment. And then the moment passed as I moved into the driver's seat.

"Ready Justin?" I yelled, looking at him.

"Ready Dad!" he yelled back. I gave the boat a little gas to take the slack out of the line, and looking back, I could see Justin ready and waiting to get up. I hit the throttle hard and he pulled right out of the water. This time he focused on keeping the skis together. He was up for about five minutes when we finally slowed down, swung around, and picked him up. He had the biggest smile on his face.

"Did you see me dad? I was skiing! That was a blast! Can we do it again?" he asked coughing out water and smiling and yelling. He was all excited about his newly developed skill.

"Just one more time around and then we'll call it a day," I said. We put Justin back in the water and gave him another ten minute ride around the lake. It was a thoroughly enjoyable day and a day my oldest son would never forget. It was something I would never forget either.

The next day at work I was remembering the events of the previous day and realized how important it was for me to create learning opportunities for my children. Teaching Justin how to ski was an accident. We were there, we had a ski boat, and I felt like he was ready for a new challenge. It wasn't a life lesson or life memory I had planned or envisioned. It just happened on its own. I made a mental note to be more mindful of ways that Mary and I could help our children succeed at the things they tried. I needed to be more purposeful about creating learning opportunities for our children.

The rest of the summer flew by with all the barbeques in the backyard, swim parties, and weekends with Mary and the kids. Work was going very well which allowed me to focus on spending time with my family. Ruth was growing every day and sometimes it was a little unsettling to see the changes happening so quickly. I spent more time with Ruth than I had with either of my boys. This was partly because I had been so busy with work before and there was more time now. Also, I knew my boy's minds pretty well and had a sixth sense about what to do with them and when to turn them over to their mother.

Ruth was different. Maybe because she was a girl and maybe for some other reason spending time with her was a mystical experience. Ruth was always "just there". She was so present and attentive and quiet and patient. It was as if she was nothing more than an observer and it seemed like she absorbed and recorded everything around her.

I'm not sure exactly how it started, but Mary and I decided our family needed a telescope. We set it up in the backyard and spent the rest of our summer nights looking at the stars and the moon and planets. Very quickly, it blossomed into a full blown study of the heavens with the boys demanding more information about what was up there. So before we knew it, our family had quite a collection of picture books showing the constellations, two books about the moon and the moon landings, three books about the Apollo space program, a pictorial essay on Jupiter, and of course, we all had NASA T-shirts.

By Christmas I had almost forgotten about my trip to Egypt and the time I spent at the Sphinx. Family life had so completely absorbed me that my time in Egypt felt more like a distant dream than something that actually happened to me. The strange thing was I could still remember every detail. The interesting thing about all of this is that, I became aware of the need to teach my children about all the earth sciences. While I'd always been good with computers and was an accomplished biotech researcher, I hadn't serious studied astronomy. Suddenly I was consumed with a thirst for knowledge about the beginning of the universe, ancient aliens, and earth history. I not only wanted to know everything about the subject, I felt compelled to discuss these subjects with my children. Somehow it became clear to me that they really needed to be good at this stuff if they were going to make it on their own in the world.

My boys learned all about astronomy. They went through all things biological with me at a time when children their age were playing marbles or video games. They were learning about the physical universe they lived in. Both boys became absorbed with geology and archeology. My children were going to be the ones that did something with their lives! I didn't know what. I had no idea at all, but I knew they would one day become famous for something they discovered. I didn't pay too much attention to Ruth as she tagged along on our little excursions. She was too small to understand any of this academic stuff, but I was wrong. Later on I would come to learn that she understood more than I gave her credit for.

Two days after Christmas I suffered a most disturbing dream. Mary and I had gone to bed and sometime after midnight I woke up terrified. I was covered in sweat and remember the whole dream. Somehow I was back with Micah and Gabe. I'm not sure where we were, but they were teaching me new things. Gabe was speaking about a new time coming to planet earth and that humankind would be entering a new era, a new age as a species. While he was speaking, the light grew very dim all around us, as if a shadow had been cast over us. Along with it came the sense of an evil presence that shot right through me… through my heart, my bones, my flesh, and my brain! It was the kind of darkness I had never known and it swallowed me up! Gabe and Micah spoke to each other in a tongue I had never heard before and Micah left us quickly.

"This was unexpected Doug. Come with me quickly," Gabe shouted as he turned and headed down a flight of stairs. I'm not sure how I was able to move. I was paralyzed with fear and believed that somehow I was moving with the strength of Gabe's presence. I followed him as we both went quickly downstairs to a small chamber. Gabe shut the door and immediately the evil was gone. Somehow the door and the room had blocked the presence from attacking us.

"What was that?" I shouted at Gabe. "What the hell was that thing?" I yelled still terrified.

"That was the evil one," Gabe said staring at me with an intensely serious look. I was terrified all over again. The look on Gabe's face and his concern for this presence unnerved me. Gabe was very powerful and huge and strong. I couldn't imagine him ever being afraid or even concerned about anyone, and here he was, visibly shaken by this presence.

"You must protect yourself from this presence Doug," Gabe said with a serious look on his face.

"How do I do that?" I asked, growing more terrified at where this conversation was going.

"The evil one has mostly left us alone, but something has drawn his attention to us and I fear he is here to disturb our program!" Gabe said with a look of deep concern on his face. "Doug, listen to me closely, you must protect yourself and your family. This evil one may have some interest in you that I do not yet understand. You must take care. You must be careful" Gabe said with an almost desperate tone in his voice. And then I woke up!

What the hell! What Gabe? What am I supposed to do? You didn't tell me what to do. I looked around the room and Mary was lying in bed next to me sleeping soundly. There was no noise in the house. I realized I had been dreaming, but it was so real. I was soaked with perspiration. I got out of bed and checked on the boys. They were okay. They were sleeping soundly. Next I checked Ruth's room. There she was sleeping like an angel. Everything was okay. Everything in the house was okay except for me. I was still in the clutches of the dream. Walking back to the bedroom in the dark I sensed I was not alone. There was something there in the dark with me. I could smell it! Then I realized there was an odor throughout my house that I hadn't smelled in a long time. I didn't know what it was. I couldn't remember when or where, but the odor began to rekindle a memory from a different time, but when? I don't know.

As I crawled back into bed I could feel the presence in the room with me. It was dark and cold and evil. What was I supposed to do? Gabe never told me what to do. How do I protect my family? How do I defend myself against this thing? I don't even know what it is! The evil seemed to have followed me right out of my dream and into my bedroom. The whole place was filled with it! There was a smell, almost a stench of filth in the air as I laid there in the dark trying to figure out how to do battle with it. All I could think was 'please God let this thing be gone from here.' I struggled and struggled and then I must have fallen asleep. When I awoke in the morning, the sun was up, and everything seemed normal again.

After my shower and breakfast, I went to work wondering what had just happened. Mary and the kids were all fine. They didn't see or hear or feel anything, but I had! Was I going crazy again?

Was this a new chapter in my crazy life? It's bad enough that I get abducted by aliens every now and then, but now there are ghosts and demons I have to contend with? My scientific world seemed to be collapsing around me as nothing made linear sense anymore. The old equations and hypotheses didn't fit the program I was involved with now. This must be something new. It's something I've never known before. I needed some secret knowledge to get a handle on my new reality.

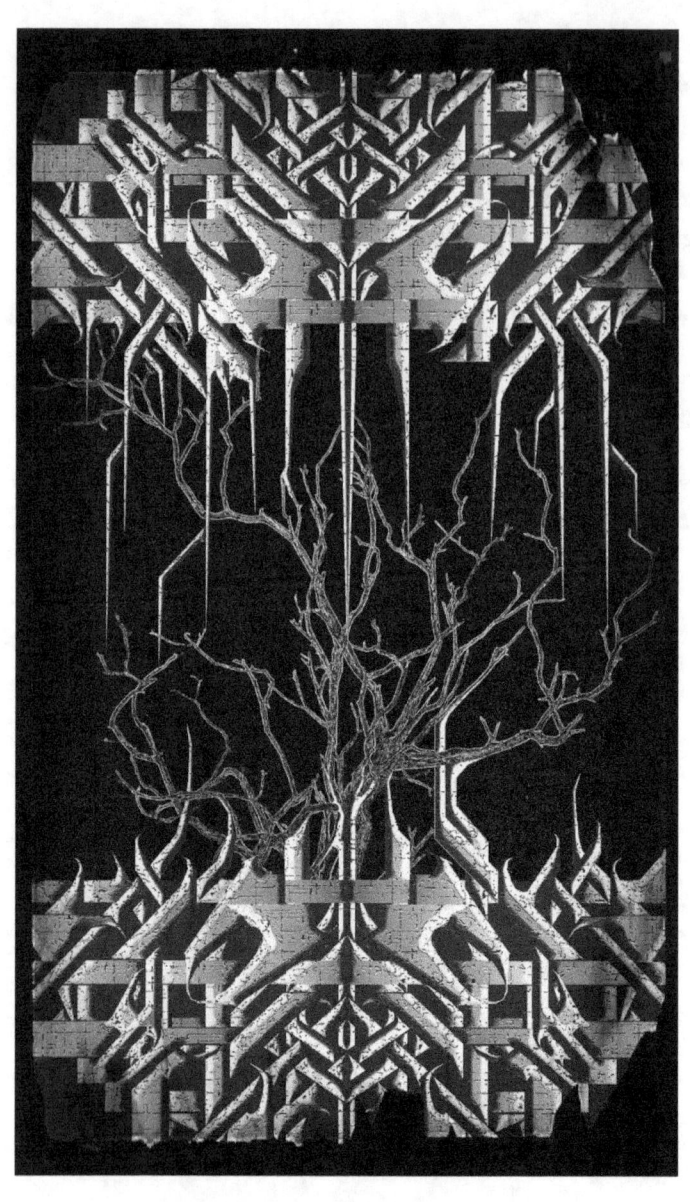

"NEURO-MECH INTERFACE"

Chapter 8

My nightmares continued for months. I felt like I was fighting dragons or vampires. For a while I let myself believe that the devil himself was coming for me and then I realized I must be going crazy. I made an appointment with my doctor to find out what was going on. After tests and discussions, Dr. Jameson said there was nothing wrong with me. He said maybe I needed some time off. There was no clinical sign of any pathology whatsoever. I was normal. This left me with the task of solving the problem on my own. Then it hit me! I realized I hadn't said a word to Mary about any of this and I decide to talk to her about it.

"Mary, I need to tell you about the nightmares I've been having," I said, opening up the conversation.

"What nightmares? You've been having nightmares?" she asked with a concerned look on her face. "Tell me about them," she said.

I began to share with her more than my nightmares. I realized that under the guise of nightmares I could begin to share with her the other stories and adventures I'd been having with the aliens. I told her everything. She listened intently to everything I had to say. She asked questions and it seemed she almost believed the reality I was sharing with her. She did not ridicule me or marginalize me in any way. She showed a genuine concern for what I was telling her and I was amazed at how intrigued she was to understand the meaning of my dreams. On more than one occasion, she would ask me to give her specific details of where I was and who was with me.

"So this evil one is some kind of demon?" she asked. "Is this something we need to concern ourselves with?" she said.

"I, I don't know. So far all of this has been like a dream to me," I said, knowing that much of it had actually happened out of time so to speak, but it had actually happened! It wasn't part of my dream world or imagination.

"And the doctors don't know what to make of it?" she asked with a puzzled look on her face.

"No. The doctor said there is nothing wrong with me." I replied.

"Well, let's hope these nightmares stop." she said with a hopeful gesture of her hands.

When Ruth turned four, there was a very unusual incident that happened. We had thrown a typical and normal birthday party for a four year old. All her little friends were there and her brothers also. It was a great time and she enjoyed herself thoroughly. It was afterwards, when I was putting her to bed that things seemed to go awry.

"Daddy, can I talk to you about something?" she asked me as I was slipping her night clothes on her.

"Of course you can honey; what's on your mind?" I asked with a smile on my face.

"I've been having bad dreams. I don't know what they mean, but they scare me. I'm afraid for you because something bad always happens to you in my dreams," she said with a very concerned look on her face.

"Honey, don't worry. We all have bad dreams sometimes, but they are only dreams. I wouldn't worry too much about them," I said reassuring her as best I could. "I'll leave the door open all night. Mommy and I are just right here," I reassured her.

"Okay daddy," she said as she snuggled down into her bed covers.

The whole episode left me undone. Now my baby was having nightmares! How do I protect her from that? How do I protect my family from anything?

It was during all this confusion and nightmares that I heard from my friend Bob.

"Hey Doug, how are you?" he said on the other end of the phone.

"I'm doing well. How are you and the family?" I asked.

"We're doing very well. I have a new job with a new company and things couldn't be better." Bob said with a confident tone in his voice.

"Wow Bob! That's really great news. I'm glad it worked out for you," I said.

"Yeah, this seems like a great company and they started me at more than I was making before, and there is room to grow with these guys. Things are looking good for me. Say, let's plan to get together sometime in the near future. Let me know when you're free for lunch and we can meet in the middle," he said laughing.

"Yeah, okay. I'll let you know when I can get away," I said, realizing that Bob had no idea what that meant to me.

A few months later Bob called and asked to meet me for lunch in Riverton. I got a sinking feeling in my stomach. If I go and meet with him, something's going to happen. I've been to Riverton many times on my own and nothing happened during those times. It's only when Bob makes a date that I get sucked out of time and end up someplace I never imagined myself to be. I really didn't want to have lunch with Bob in Riverton ever again!

"Yeah Bob! Sure Riverton on Tuesday at noon for lunch. You got it," I said and hung up the phone. WOW. Here I go again. The nightmares had stopped for months now, but my life was no longer my own. There were too many loose ends and now my baby was having nightmares and I was powerless to stop them. All I could ever do was to hold her and comfort her as best I could. I felt so helpless against this new darkness that had invaded our home. What was I going to do? What was happening to me and my family?

I let Mary know that I was only going to work half a day and that I'd be meeting Bob in Riverton for lunch. She reminded me to say hi and find out about the babies and how they were doing. As I pulled into the parking lot at Denny's in Riverton, I felt relieved that it was actually Denny's. As I walked inside, Bob was already there and had secured a booth for us.

"What's up Bob? I said with a big smile of relief on my face. Bob was beaming! Maybe this won't be so bad after all.

"Hi Doug. Hey buddy, I'm glad to see you! I just wanted to share the good news of my new job. It's a wonderful company and my boss is the coolest guy in the world! He's a little strange sometimes, but he has a heart of gold. And he actually talks to me and listens to my ideas. I owe it all to you!" Bob said with a huge smile.

"What do you mean Bob? What did I do?" I asked. The waiter came and we ordered lunch when Bob responded.

"Well when they interviewed me, I gave them your name as a reference, and they must have done their research, because Walter, my new boss, talked to your boss, who gave you a glowing review. I think it's what decided the job for me," Bob said smiling and a little calmer.

"Tell me more. Did he say what my boss said about me?" I asked waiting to hear what Bob had to say.

The waiter came and brought our coffee, took our order, and vanished.

"He didn't say, except that after talking to your boss, Walter looked at me and said he thought I was the person he needed for the position!"

"He asked about you! He seemed to know a lot about you and your family and wanted to know all about our friendship and high school and stuff. I thought that was a little strange. For a minute it felt like Walter was thinking about offering you a job as well. Then, once I got settled in, he fired like 3-4 people all around me. They were just gone for no apparent reason. He said he needed new blood in the organization. Then he hired new people that don't seem to know much about our business, but he likes them. I'm not sure what any of it means. It's all a little odd to me," Bob said with a concerned look on his face.

"How does he know me? Why is he interested in my family," I asked with concerns of my own.

"He said that during his conversation with your boss that your boss was describing some of his staff and your name came up. Your boss told my boss that you've been a great asset to the success of your company. I'm not sure what else he might have said about you," Bob shared. "He's a very likable man, but also seems a little quirky sometimes. I can't put my finger on it, but sometimes he seems like he's two different people," Bob said, looking off into space. Bob shared with me some of the more routine aspects of his new job and he also filled me in on how well his family is doing.

I kept trying to steer the conversation back to his boss, but as I started, the waiter returned with our food and Bob excused himself to use the restroom. When he returned I realized I needed to go as well. I didn't want to go, but I couldn't hold it anymore, so I went to the restroom. When I opened the restroom door I was relieved to walk back into Denny's and saw Bob sitting there taking a bite from his burger.

"There you are!" Bob said. "I started to worry where you went."

"Was I gone that long?" I asked.

"Yeah, about ten minutes. Are you okay? " Bob asked.

"So tell me again Bob, why is your boss so interested in me?" I asked.

"Well, I almost think he would like to hire you, but he didn't say that. Also it might be due to the big project they just assigned me to," Bob added.

"What kind of project?" I asked.

"We've been working on a big project. Actually it was a big project before they hired me, but Jim, one of my bosses, said he needed my help on it. But sometimes I get the feeling that I'm not totally on their team. They involve me and then they keep sections of the project from me. I mean, I'm not supposed to talk about this stuff, but it's pretty cutting edge material."

"What's the project?" I asked.

"Well, we're working on an artificial intelligence program that we hope can be integrated into the Internet. The program was designed to collect data using a new set of algorithms. Jim says this project will create a next generation search engine. It will help users make more intelligent choices when they are online and connect them more deeply to the Internet," Bob shared.

"It sounds very cool!" I said.

"Yeah, well you haven't seen the plans or the scope of service this thing is designed to perform." Bob added in. "The name of the software is called N.O.A.H. It stands for New Order of Artificial Human! Pretty bizarre huh? The system has optical recognition and can see us. It has a voice and can speak. It's very strange when you start talking with "NOAH".

"That's really very cool Bob. I mean you could be doing something meaningless, but you're working on a revolutionary machine, one that can help move society light years ahead of where we are now." I said.

"It's strange that you're doing that kind of work. My company has been involved with several projects that involve Genome sequencing. I know our company's' are in different fields, but some of what we are doing in my company is every bit as exciting as what you're working on," I said.

"We've been working on a big project as well. Of course we perform a variety of genome sequencing programs targeting several different human diseases as well as searching for ways to regenerate different types of tissues like skin, hair, eyes, bone, and some of the major organs. We've been working on this project to regenerate brain cells, which is very exciting and we've actually had some success!" I said with a sense of pride. Doug finished his sandwich and didn't respond, so I changed the subject.

"So when are we getting together?" I said. The course change caught Bob completely off guard.

"What do you mean?" he asked.

"I mean, when can your family and my family get together for a BBQ and maybe a movie or something?" I asked with a smile.

"Oh! Hey that sounds like a great idea. Maybe next month we can plan something. How about setting a date sometime in the next four to five weeks?" Bob suggested.

"Let me check my calendar for a good date and also check with the wife. If my calendar is open, then we're on!" I said.

Bob and I finished our lunch and I was on my way home. How many times have I done this trip? I was basking in the quiet joy of actually going to Riverton and having lunch with Bob at Denny's. No aliens!

As I pulled into the driveway, Mary came out to meet me. She gave me a very big hug and said:

"I'm so glad your home! I'm so glad you're safe and home!" with an expression of concern on her face.

"What's the matter honey?" I asked, letting her pull away from me.

"Let's go inside and I'll explain," Mary said.

We went inside and sat in the living room. "I've been talking with Ruth and she had some very strange things to tell me. I'm worried about her." Mary said.

"What has she been saying?" I asked.

"Well, when I got her up from her nap this afternoon, she started telling me she had been with you and Gabe! I asked her how she knew Gabe and she said he was a very nice man that was her friend and also daddy's friend. She said Gabe was going to help us to do something. She didn't know exactly what you were going to do, but she was adamant that Gabe was going to help you both. I don't know what it means," Mary said.

"Mary, it sounds like Ruth is having bad dreams like me. Maybe she heard us talking. Maybe she heard me mention Gabe's name. I've never said a word to the kids about any of this stuff. If it would make you feel better, I can take her to see Dr. Jameson," I said, not knowing what else to say or do.

"THE ARCHITECT OF DREAMS | BOU RATTAT"

Chapter 9

Two weeks later my boss, Rick Flannigan, called me in to his office.

"Doug, we have an important meeting coming up in a couple of weeks. We are meeting a potential new client from down south. His name is Walter Harrison and he's the CEO of Galaxy Industries. They want to discuss a business proposition regarding some of our genomic research. Mr. Harrison has been spearheading a new project and feels they can use our help with the genomics side of the equation. I don't have many details, but wanted to give you a heads up. Soon as I get more details we'll meet and prepare for the meeting."

"Wow! Sounds like it could be a good piece of new business for us. Hey, I have a friend that works at Galaxy. He hasn't been there that long. Maybe I should call him and see if I can get some details," I said.

"No Doug. Don't do that. I think that might spook them. Besides, I already know about your friend Bob. Walter Harrison called me and asked a lot of questions about you! He said your friend Bob gave your name as a reference. Don't worry. I said good things about you. So, don't call Bob. Let's just wait and see what Mr. Harrison gives us to work with," Rick said.

"Agreed," I said. "Thanks for the information boss. I'm looking forward to the meeting." I left Rick's office and wanted to call Bob, but resisted the temptation. We needed the new business and the last thing I needed was to screw it up with my friendship with Bob. Well, at least I'll get the chance to meet Bob's new boss and make my own decisions about him.

At the end of the week Rick called me into his office again.

"Doug, here's the information from Galaxy. I just got off the phone with Walter Harrison and he already sent me the data files he'd like us to review for the meeting. I'll forward you a copy of everything. Maybe you can get started on it this weekend. If we both jump on this we can meet on Monday or Tuesday at the latest and draw up a game plan," Rick said.

"Right boss, I'll study it over the weekend and be ready on Monday," I said.

By the time I got home the files were in my email. I said hello to Mary and the kids and went directly into my study. As I reviewed file after file I became aware that the information I was reviewing was what Bob had briefly described to me. This was the 'N.O.A.H. project.' The more I studied it, the more I came to appreciate its subtle elegance. It was absolutely brilliant! By the time I finished reviewing the last file, I couldn't wait to meet NOAH in person. If this stuff is all true, if they are actually doing this now…the future is truly here! The possibilities are endless for what NOAH could do for humanity. I wasn't sure how my firm came into play on this deal though.

I can understand an artificial intelligence interface with the Internet that is capable of "thinking", remembering, and even predicting a million billion details in real time, but where do the genomics come in? The meeting next week would be very interesting. I couldn't wait to meet Mr. Harrison and find out what part my firm will play in his new program.

On Monday, Rick and I reviewed the details that we received from Mr. Harrison. Neither of us could figure out why he needed our expertise in his project. Obviously Mr. Harrison had left out a few key details that I'm sure he would reveal at our meeting at the end of the week. Neither Rick nor I could really focus on our regular work all week. Rick had set the meeting up with Mr. Harrison and his project manager for Friday. We'd meet in the morning around ten AM, chat for a bit, have lunch, dive into the meat and potatoes of the project in the afternoon, and then finish with a nice dinner.

On Friday morning Rick and I were both nervous as we waited for ten A.M. and the arrival of our guests. When they arrived I was surprised to see Bob with him. Bob was the project manager!

"Mr. Harrison! So pleased to meet you," Rick said as he extended his hand. Both men shook hands and exchanged warm and broad smiles.

"Bob Smith", Bob said, shaking Rick's hand.

"Mr. Harrison, so nice to meet you," I said shaking his hand. "I'm Doug Keller."

"Doug Keller! It's a pleasure to meet you after all the good things I've heard about you. I'm not sure if Rick has told you, but I hired your friend Bob here based on my conversation with Rick...about you! For that matter, that's one of the reason's we're here today. When our project ran into roadblocks, I remembered my conversation with Rick and well, here we are," he said with a warm smile.

"Why thank you very much, Mr. Harrison," I said, a little embarrassment at the compliment.

"Hi Bob. What a pleasant surprise to see you here," I added.

"Hi Doug. It's great to be here and good to see you. How's the family?" he asked.

"Great! They're all doing just great. How's everyone in your family?"

"I can't complain. They're all healthy and busy doing what they do," Bob replied.

"Well, let's go into my office and get started, shall we?" Rick asked, gesturing us all toward his office.

"Do either of you need to use the restroom before we begin? You guys have been on the road for a while, you might want to use the facilities," Rick said.

"No. I'm fine," Bob said.

"Me too," Mr. Harrison said. With that we all moved into the conference room in Rick's office and began the long awaited discussion.

"So tell us Mr. Harrison, what is your vision for this project?" Rick started.

"Let me begin by explaining: this project has been a long time coming. There have been millions of technical details that needed to be worked out and put in place before we could begin this phase of the project. We believe we are finally ready for phase two," Mr. Harrison stated.

"Our vision has been to harness the exquisite power of artificial intelligence and to make it serve our needs. We are at a point in our global civilization where technology must be used to manage the vast knowledge we are discovering every day. We believe NOAH can help us with that problem. The vision actually has two goals: The first goal is to create a platform on the Internet that will generate revenue by serving everyone that uses the Internet. There are an infinite number of personal services that can be offered and performed once we know the specific needs and requirements of a user. We have developed our own quantum computer that will handle all transactions," Mr. Harrison stopped talking and looked around the room.

"We've assembled a team of extraordinary computer scientists. Collectively, they've written brilliant code and algorithms for NOAH. This programming will allow him to collate vast amounts of data in real time, and here's the best part: he will be able to make decisions regarding the importance of the value of the data!" Mr. Harrison explained.

"Our second goal is much more ambitious. We expect to create a computer that is augmented with a biological human host that will usher in a new age of trans-humanism. Our creation will establish a plethora of new and innovative techniques to fuse electromechanical components with human biology," Walter explained, pausing for us to grasp what he was saying.

"Our team has struggled with the neural plasticity dynamics of creating NOAH's synthetic neural network. We've been very successful in developing algorithms to serve the neural net mapping sequences necessary for NOAH to study and learn to replicate the smallest detail of each system he studies. The tricky part for us has been trying to achieve the intended results without any biology. We now believe it may be decades before we make the breakthrough using only programming. If we could develop a biological model for NOAH to learn from, we believe our progress will shorten that time to months or perhaps weeks!

In short, we need a human brain to make everything work as we've planned," Mr. Harrison said looking down with an uncomfortable expression on his face.

"We've beta tested NOAH and he is able to handle every task we've given him, but we are looking to take our project one step further. NOAH operates on our quantum computer. The system is cutting edge stuff! The platform itself is exquisite in every detail. The genius of the project resides in a very tiny microchip and can be inserted into a human brain. Our intention has been to interface NOAH with a human being. That pathway appeared to be the most logical and having the fewest technological hurdles. Our testing of this smaller unit using Wi-Fi has been very promising so far. The two units communicate with each other and once connected never lose connection. Our hope was we can develop a biological host for NOAH's "brain."

"There's only one problem to our plan: I can't get past the ethical aspects of such a project," Mr. Harrison said with a sad and serious look on his face. Our team has wrestled with this issue for month now, and well, it's my money and I can't stomach the idea of using a real human for the project. I'm not Dr. Frankenstein!" he said with a powerful stare.

"There is really no ethical path for us. We cannot use any part of a living sentient being in our project. When we started the project our goal was to create a synthetic neural network to support the AI aspects of the project. We were shooting to create a program or programs that would create something like, well, like...NOAH! The problems began piling up a while back. Several months ago our team of programmers admitted they were years away from a software solution. That brings us to you folks," Mr. Harrison said.

"I don't follow. How can we help you? We're a biotech company," Rick said.

"We want you to construct a biological brain for us. It would not be a person. It wouldn't have a soul. It would be the biological component of our system," Mr. Harrison explained.

"You want us to do what?" Rick said, choking on his words.

"That's impossible! It can't be done. We certainly don't have the knowledge or technology to create such a thing," Rick explained, turning red and gasping for air.

"We are not talking about a whole brain Rick. We have some ideas we'd like to run past you and your team to see if your genomics department can help us to develop some of these living tissues. I have my own team that will do the rest," Mr. Harrison added.

"I seriously doubt my firm can help you Mr. Harrison," Rick relied sternly. The look on Rick's face told me he could see this new project slipping away from us.

"Think of the possibilities of creating the most powerful computer ever known and combining it with the best aspects of a human brain! NOAH, the computer portion, would have a biological custodian or caretaker for the entire program! Of course NOAH would not have anything like free will. He would not be a sentient being at all. NOAH is a computer, but his biological counterpart would be, what we envision is a very elegant bio-robot. For all practical purposes it would look human and act human, but would be the technical link between us and the mainframe. Noah's smaller unit can be programmed with linguistics programs which allow us to talk to him. We can give him commands and have him run the calculations and probabilities for success. He becomes our physical assistant in managing Internet traffic! Can you imagine the possibilities of such a creature? It's enormous!" Mr. Harrison finished. He was aglow with what he had just shared with us.

I looked over at Rick. He was mesmerized as we all were. This would be a phenomenal leap forward in both science, technology, and of course, genomics. Everyone sat there for a few minutes, silently calculating what we were just now understanding and imagining the possibilities for a brave new future for us all. I could see that Rick was calculating the many possibilities of this project. After about three or four minutes he spoke up.

"Mr. Harrison, I must say that your project is very ambitious and possibly overreaching, but it's intriguing as well. I can't promise you we will succeed. Trust and integrity are critical elements in our business and I would be less than honest if I promised you we could deliver on this project. I can promise that, if we decide to join you, that we will give our very best effort toward the goals," Rick said.

Rick continued, "We have several programs that can address many of your technical issues. We believe we can deliver acceptable supports for your program. Of course we have limited understanding of the interaction between the biological and the computer brain. Do you have research on this relationship? Have you thought out how such a relationship will work or can work?" Rick asked.

"Yes, actually we have developed a theoretical understanding of what we can expect regarding the bio-technical interface. We've developed a kind of synthetic neural network for NOAH. It's completely artificial; however, we believe it will marry up with the biological systems. At least that is our hope. There is still much we don't know as we don't have the expertise your firm possesses. That's why we need your help in this project. Will you help us? Can you help us?" Mr. Harrison asked showing some tension for the first time.

"I honestly don't know Mr. Harrison," Rick replied. "I'm fascinated with your progress and development of a synthetic neural network. I would need to see more. Doug and I both have studied the data you sent me, but I need more information. I need to see more data and then, maybe we can begin to propose a bridge or intersection of biological/human and machine. This is absolutely fascinating stuff. We need to work out the details and the funding requirements, but we are definitely interested in partnering in this project." Rick said emphatically.

"Please let me confer with my staff when I return to my office. We may have some additional information to share with you," Mr. Harrison replied.

"Great!" Rick said.

"Shall we have some lunch?" Mr. Harrison proposed.

We broke for lunch. After lunch we spent the rest of the day hammering out the details of the scheduled deliveries required to keep the project moving forward. Dinner was an interesting time. I watched and listened to Mr. Harrison the whole evening. He was an interesting man. If I had to describe him, I'd say he

129

was a compassionate visionary. All evening he kept mentioning how much this project could help people all over the world. On the front side, NOAH would help connect people that needed to be connected and would contribute to flowing information where it was needed most. This would all happen in real time, so there would be no lag-time. Information and support would be instantaneous! Mr. Harrison was dazzling all of us with his brilliant insights into the future of technology and biology and appeared to be a solid visionary humanitarian. I was sold and felt like Rick was sold as well.

The next day Rick put me in charge of the project.

 "I want you to give this project your full attention. You are relieved from all your other projects. This project will be the project that puts us in the international market," Rick said with a wild look of enthusiasm. "This is the break our company has been looking for Doug and you are the guy that can deliver it. Let's meet next week to review our research projects and rank the inventory so we know what we have to offer Galaxy." Rick said.

By ten AM Rick received the email with the additional data for the NOAH project. He printed out two copies and forwarded me the electronic file. The rest of the day was spent pouring over the data from all the sub-projects. There were many pages of documents illustrating the clinical trials and experiments their team had performed.

"This data is incredible!" Rick said with a look of wonder on his face.

"Doug, if this guy's data is correct, the implication for what we can do to help people is astronomical! If we can deliver on our side of the equation we will be able to offer humans a variety of choices regarding their healthcare needs and maybe even their mortality! Do you see that in the data Doug?" Rick asked, smiling with growing excitement.

"I do! It's truly amazing what these guys have developed Rick. They've got ninety five percent of the work completed, but I can see a couple of roadblocks. I guess that's where we come in," I said.

"Exactly!" said Rick.

The following week I received a card in the mail from Mr. Harrison thanking me for my time at the meeting and looking forward to working together on the new project. The whole thing was very exciting. Rick had promised me a big raise and a fat bonus if we delivered on this new contract. Not only was it going to be fun working with Bob, I was going to get a big raise out of the deal!

It had been a long time since my last meeting with Gabe. Part of me was concerned that I hadn't been contacted and part of me was more excited about this new project at work. These were confusing times for me. I had waited my whole career for an assignment like this and even a fading memory of my time with the aliens seemed to pale against this new challenge. My days now were consumed with wild ideas and searching to find solutions to the roadblocks in the project. I couldn't stop my mind from hashing and rehashing the data and creating wildly imaginative scenes of ways to envision how a machine and a person could interact and operate as a single organism. I could see such incredible possibilities for the success of this project and how it would set up a new wave of cutting edge technology for humanity.

The phone rang and I answered it, but wasn't prepared for the voice on the other end. "Hello." I said.

"Is this Doug?" the voice on the other end asked.

"Yes. This is Doug."

"Hi Doug, this is Walter Harrison."

"Mr. Harrison! What a pleasant surprise. How are you?" I asked slightly stunned.

"Please call me Walter, Doug. I'm fine. I was just in town and wanted to see if you were available for us to meet briefly? I'm sorry to spring this on you, but it occurred to me as I was finishing up my business that I may have some additional information that's going to help you and Rick accelerate your timeline on your project. I thought that might interest you and would be a great help to me. Can we meet somewhere?" he asked.

"Well yes. Yes we can meet. When? Where? I need to let my wife know I'll be going out."

"How about the Wellington Hotel lobby, say in an hour," Walter said.

"That works for me. I'll see you in an hour." Just as I hung up the phone Mary came into the room.

"Who was that?" she asked.

"That was Walter Harrison! He's in town and wants to meet with me right now. Can you believe it?" I was in a state of shock.

"Are you going? Where is it? Is Rick meeting with you as well?" Mary asked.

"I, I don't know if Rick will be there or not. Mr. Harrison didn't say," I replied. "I'll be back in a few hours," I said. I gave Mary a quick kiss and drove to the hotel.

Walter Harrison was sitting in one of the big lobby chairs. I walked over and smiled.

"Mr. Harrison. Good to see you sir," I said.

"Thank you for coming on such short notice Doug, and please call me Walter," he said.

"I was reviewing some of my notes for a meeting I had earlier today and realized that I have some additional information for you and Rick. It hadn't occurred to me before that you would need this information so early on, but, after thinking it all through, I realized that this could help you both on your end," he added.

"Here, let's move over here to this table for a bit more privacy. Would you like something from the bar?" he asked.

"No. No thank you. I'm fine," I said.

"Good. Well what I want to share with you in plain English is that we've made extraordinary progress is developing nearly functional synthetic axons. It would probably be more accurate to call them axon connectors as their duel function is to bridge the gap between the electronics and the biological elements. We've been experimenting with several prototypes expecting to find the right one that will reliably fire every single time. We've learned there are very subtle biorhythm frequencies present that

133

must be calibrated precisely to encourage their biological counterparts to connect and communicate with each other. We think we've solved that and this issue will be one of our first hurdles," he explained.

"You mean the synthetic axons can make a positive connection with your biological dendrites?" I asked in disbelief.

"Yes, precisely! We believe we have found a process that creates the conditions for this to take place. It's all here in the data. I want you and Rick to have it. Please review it and call me or Bob if you have any questions. We are eager to get started and need this project to go smoothly. We all have deadlines and I want to insure we all meet the deadlines," he said.

"I've also included a file detailing our algorithms to manage the neural plasticity aspects of the union and a small section on neural mapping," Walter added.

That was it! It took less than ten minutes for Walter to explain himself and his discoveries. They were fabulous and simple and elegant as nature herself. It seemed a little awkward now that we arrived at the point of our meeting so quickly. Was there nothing else to discuss? I realized that I had absolutely nothing to say to him regarding the project. I hadn't even gotten started really.

"How's your family Doug? I'm sorry to pull you away from them so quickly, but I felt this was too important to wait until next week. Do you have children?" he asked.

"Yes. I have three children; two boys and a little girl," I replied.

"How about you Mr., I mean Walter. Do you have children?"

"No Doug. Unfortunately I don't. My wife died many years ago and we never had children. After her death, it didn't seem important to have children. It took a great while for me to get over her death and well, by the time I moved on, I never managed to find the right woman, the type that I wanted to get involved with, let alone, to have my children. It simply didn't happen for me and now, well here I am!" he explained. "

My wife died young of a rare cancer. It was devastating to me to lose her that way. Since then, I mean after my grieving had become manageable, I promised that I would spend every last nickel I had and every ounce of energy I could muster to develop cures for these diseases that plague us all," Walter said. We sat there for a few moments in silence and then he spoke again.

"So how old are your boys?" Walter asked.

"Justin is almost eight years old and Doug Junior is almost six. My little girl Ruth is four," I added.

"Is there much difference between raising boys and raising girls? Walter asked.

"Well, yes there is and maybe no also. I mean, I have different activities with the boys than I do with my little girl, but I love them all the same and they all have to live by the same rules. Yeah, there is a difference," I finished

"Tell me about your little girl. Is she going to be a scientist like her dad or will she grow up to be more like her mother?" Walter asked.

"It's hard to tell when they're so young. I mean, Ruth is 100% her mother. There's no doubt about that, but Ruth and I have our time together and we enjoy some of the same things. I guess we'll just have to wait and see what she decides! Isn't that pretty much how life plays out?" I said.

"I'd like to meet your family sometime Doug. I always feel closer to the people I'm working with once I've met their family. Maybe we could arrange a get together sometime with, you know Bob and his family and also Rick and his family. Maybe we could have a BBQ in the park or something. What do you think?" Walter asked.

"That's a great idea Walter! Just let me know a good date and time and we'll make it happen," I said.

"Great Doug! Well I've kept you from your family long enough. You should probably be getting back. I think we made solid progress here today. We'll plan to talk at our mid-week teleconference."

"Thank you for your time Walter. I really am glad you called me today. The information you gave me will help us move quickly in the next two to four weeks," I added.

"Until next week Doug."

"Thank you sir, I look forward to our meeting next week."

By the time I got home I had played and replayed the new information in my head. It was great information! What I didn't share with Walter was what we had discovered during one of our latest experiments. The results of this latest experiment would help us over-deliver on our timeline and move the project into phase two ahead of schedule. My firm had been working on a process that assists the dendrites and axons to make connections very quickly. We had also stumbled upon information that would help us create a process to multiply the number of axons and the dendrite connections! Our number to hit was 500 million pattern recognitions in a single brain! It would be a significant leap forward if we could hit that number and hopefully will help to improve cognitive functions, Alzheimer's disease, and Dementia. That's our hope anyway.

When I got home Mary was upset. "What's going on Mary?" I asked.

"It's Ruth. She woke up from her nap screaming and terrified! I asked her what was wrong and all she could say was, "They're coming! They're coming mommy!"

"Who's coming? " I asked in a panic.

"I don't know. Ruth couldn't tell me. She said she didn't know either!" Mary replied. Mary's words shocked me as I tried to remain calm.

"Well, it was probably just a bad dream," I said trying to calm my wife. "I'll talk with her in a bit," I said.

"Do you think it was 'them'?" Mary asked.

"You mean the aliens? I don't know. I don't think so," I said. Those were the first words I heard Dr. Frankenstein speak so long ago. 'They're coming!' I had to wonder what this meant. Of course this had everything to do with the aliens, but I didn't want Mary thinking such things and worrying about it. I had been so wrapped up in this new project at work I had put the whole alien program on hold and not thought about it much. Now I needed to try and contact Gabe. But how do I do that? How do I give him a call?

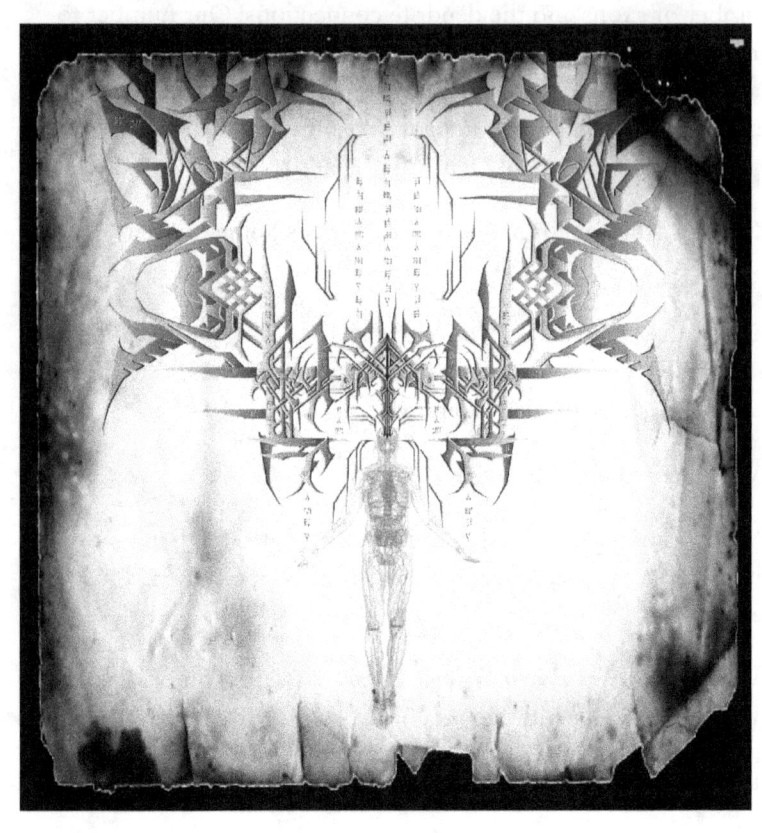

"ASCENSION"

Chapter 10

"Doug this is Bob. How are you guys doing?" he asked.

"We're coming along Bob. Testing is going very well. How are things on your end?" I asked, wondering what was on Bob's mind.

"We're good to go on our end. That's why I called. Walter and Jim asked me to arrange a face to face with you later this week. I thought we could make it easy on both of us and meet in Riverton. Does that work for you? I was thinking we could have lunch on Friday," Bob said.

"Yeah, I guess I can do that. I'll meet you at Denny's in Riverton on Friday. Is that the plan?" I asked, still wary of going to Riverton for anything except to fill the gas tank at the highway gas station.

"That's the plan Doug! I'll see you on Friday. I'll bring the new data and two schedule changes," Bob said and hung up.

I pulled into Denny's on Friday about a quarter to noon. Bob's car was already in the parking lot. I walked in and saw Bob siting in our normal booth.

"Hey buddy! Thanks for coming," he said with a big smile.

"Hi Bob. How are things at Galaxy? You guys ready for the big trials coming up?" I said slipping into the booth.

"We're ready to go Doug. Walter thought it was important for us to talk and he wanted me to give you and Rick some additional thoughts our team has developed," Bob said.

The waiter interrupted us, took our order and disappeared. A minute later he came back with two coffees. Looking at my coffee I realized I need to get rid of the cup of coffee I drank in the car on the way down here.

"I'll be right back Bob. I've got to use the restroom," I said.

When I walked out of the restroom my heart sank. I had walked smack into the middle of Emma's and there was Micah sitting at the counter. It felt strange and familiar at the same time.

"Hi Micah," I said with a tone that was almost disappointing.

"We have some serious work to do Doug. Gabe is waiting for us," he said. With that, we entered the walk-in box and were off.

"Where are we off to this time Micah? I asked.

"Machu Picchu," Micah replied. We were soon very high in the sky. It wasn't long before we could see the Andes Mountains in front of us and were coming down right above Machu Picchu. Once again, there was the familiar hum and then somehow we flew right into the ruins and stopped just inside the mountain. When we stopped and the doors of the cold box opened, I could hardly believe what I saw. It was a whole new world I had stepped into! This was the third time I had experienced this routine, but it was all so stunning and exhilarating.

The whole place was alive. I could feel it vibrating all around me. The air was different, the trees and skies looked different from any of the other places they had taken me. It was a jungle scene, but it didn't look like any jungle I had ever seen before, not even on the moon, or in Egypt! I could see birds and animals moving around in the jungle and in the tree branches. They were all very exotic looking creatures…almost mythical. Yes! This place had a mythical feeling about it. I was as if this place existed in its own dimension.

We walked through the jungle for a ways and came to a clearing and a group of huts. There was one big hut in the middle and Micah steered us toward the big one. I wasn't prepared for what I saw inside. My heart stopped! I couldn't breathe for a minute. In the middle of the room was Gabe, but sitting next to him was Ruth…my daughter Ruth! Why was she here? How was she here? Instantly my heart was racing and this whole alien thing became very personal for me.

"What the hell is going on here Gabe? Ruth! What are you doing here? Why is this happening?" I blurted out all in about three seconds. Even Gabe's presence couldn't stop my emotions and the fear racing through me. I was starting to get my breath when Gabe finally spoke.

"Doug, this situation is worse than we feared. Your daughter Ruth may be in danger and we need to make plans to protect her. That's why I arranged this meeting with you," he said very calmly.

"Gabe, why is my daughter here? She's so young. She shouldn't be involved in any of this stuff," I said with a frantic gasp in my voice.

Ruth sat quietly and calmly as she always does watching Gabe and I discussing the situation. Gabe looked at both of us and seemed to know things about our situation that he hadn't shared. He sat there looking and said nothing. I didn't know what to say, so I just sat there as well. Surprisingly it was Ruth who spoke first.

"Daddy, there is something I'm supposed to do, but it won't happen for a long time," she said, looking up at me with a look of complete understanding.

"What do you mean baby?" I asked.

"I have something I have to do someday. I'm not sure what it is, but I know I have to do it. I need you to help me daddy. I won't be able to do it by myself. I need you to teach me so I can get ready for it," she said. And there it was before me. I looked at Gabe and he looked at me. All the pieces began to come together for me in that moment.

"You've been training me, so I can train her!" I said angrily. "You knew! You always knew this day would come. Why didn't you tell me? Why don't I know what we're doing? What is going on Gabe? What am I doing? What is this all about? I need to know. My family is involved now. Please tell me," I said with a sense of desperation setting in.

My mind drifted back to Mary and the boys and Ruth. I remembered all of us being on the water on the lake. I thought of all our times together and our life together in the real world. Instantly I resented my relationship with the aliens. This arrangement with them had always been my problem, but now my little girl was involved! What drama had we been sucked into? Why was my little girl here? What did she have to do with any of this stuff, with these aliens, with the fate of the world? My head began spinning with the meaning of things like a centrifuge spinning out the truth. What did it all mean? I didn't know. I didn't have a clue what this all meant.

Gabe sat quietly for a long time before he spoke. He looked at me thoughtfully and said:

"Doug, we've been waiting for you for a long time. You have a strength and power we need for the work we are doing. We believed the work that will come would have been done by you. When Ruth was born, we became aware of her incredible powers. She is a very gifted child. She is one who will also make a difference in the world. This work that must be done someday can and will be done by Ruth, but it is very dangerous and we need your help. She needs your help!" Gabe said with a very serious look on his face.

"Doug, every living being has an aura around them. Your aura is a light signature that is invisible to most people, but there are a few people who have learned to see auras. This comes very easy to us, but for humans, it is much more difficult. A person's aura is affected by their birth. It is also predicated on who they are as a person and how open their mind is to the possibility of all things. There is another aspect of the properties of mind. A closed mind will not allow much light to enter the spirit. The light is always there, always available, but most people choose to ignore it and never even try. From the moment she was born, Ruth has been opened up to the light, and even now, she continues to absorb more and more light from the universe. She has a gift!" Gabe shared.

"I'm not sure I understand Gabe. An aura? What does it do? How does it work?" I asked.

"Let me try to explain it in another way. All matter is energy and it vibrates with a specific frequency. Rocks vibrate with a lower frequency than trees. Light vibrates with a higher frequency than people. All humans have an aura, but each person's aura is different. These differences can be understood and interpreted to suggest different vibrational frequencies. A person with a bright aura will be able to develop stronger connections with the universe and exert more influence on the world around them. They are better connected to the whole!" Gabe explained.

"Ruth has a very strong aura. As she grows, it will grow stronger and stronger. She has the capacity and potential to bring great changes to your planet. The question is: will her father help her?" Gabe asked staring at me.

"Of course I will help. I have to help! This is my little girl we're talking about here," I said angrily. "Why am I here? Why are we here? Why did you bring us here?" I asked, challenging Gabe's motives.

"Things have changed since we last spoke. Very bad things have happened. The evil one has returned to this planet and he brings powerful forces with him," Gabe said.

"The evil one is back? You've got to be kidding me? Gabe I've been having nightmares for months and I even had one dream and you were in it! In the dream you talked about an evil one and now you're saying this guy's real? There is a real "evil one? What kind of bad guy is he? Is he hungry for power and aims to dominate the planet and my little girl and I are supposed to stop him?" I said firing a volley of questions at Gabe.

It unraveled me to realize my deepest fears… fears that had stalked me in my sleep. The nightmares had been bad enough, but now they were coming true! How did Gabe and the aliens get into my dreams? And what do my dreams mean? Can my dreams somehow foreshadow what's going to happen soon? I couldn't believe how this could happen.

"This evil one, of which we speak, is a very ancient soul. He is old and wise and very powerful. You cannot kill him! He is an immortal. He has no need for money or gold or even fame and glory. There is only one thing ever on his mind: to collect human souls! He understands the cosmic value of human consciousness and how the soul survives after death. His aim is to steal the souls of the living before they die so he can steal their consciousness. His ultimate goal is to harness the power of that consciousness. He has plans of his own for the future of the universe." Gabe shared with a faraway look in his eyes. "I have fought with him in the past and now here he is again. His aim is to derail the changes that are coming."

"We can't kill him? Gabe, what do you mean we can't kill him? How do we stop him? What are we supposed to do? How do we fight him?" I pleaded wanting to know some advantage, some weakness, something we can do to protect ourselves.

Gabe looked at me with pity in his eyes and said:

"The invisible must be understood by the visible. This thing that must be accomplished must be an invisible thing. The invisible can influence the visible. It is an extraordinary thing in itself, in its manifestations and meaning for all time. The human species lives in the crucible of all creation. The direction of the entire universe depends upon how your people will use the power of their consciousness to influence the world around them. You already have forged weapons against this evil in your heart, but you don't know it yet. You don't know how to wield

145

the weapon. That is why you are here this time. That is why "she" is here with us this time. Together you will both learn what you need to know to defeat this evil one," Gabe said.

"You just said he couldn't be killed! Now you saying you want my daughter and me to defeat him! How can we do that?" I asked thoroughly confused at Gabe's words.

"Defeat is not the same as death. He can be thwarted from his purpose. He can be put off. He's been defeated many times in the past. My kind and I have fought with him and his minions for a very long time. He is one of the reasons I've been sent here to your planet," Gabe explained. His eyes were glowing like a hot fire.

Gabe sat silent for a long time. I didn't know what to say so I sat there quietly and contemplated our next discussion, the next lesson. I looked at little Ruth sitting quietly watching us, studying the both of us and I could tell, even now, she was learning new things. At last, Gabe spoke:

"Doug, the time has come for you to know of things that have not yet happened, but are coming. The earth is changing and all the people on earth will soon begin to experience a gigantic shift in awareness. This is something that has been developing for centuries. The catalyst for change has never quite taken hold enough to bring the change we need. There have been many people over the centuries who have pointed to it, written about it, dreamed about it, and even lived it, but it has never happened yet. But now, it will happen soon. Very soon, humankind will begin to wake up from their dream. They will slowly begin to realize they are connected. Their ultimate reality is not as billions and billions of individuals, but their future and their present will begin to manifest itself as "the one.""

"They will come to understand that they are all connected on very deep levels and what happens to one of them happens to all of them. The day is coming when they will no longer want war. They will begin to nurture each other knowing that the karma they are creating now will either hurt or benefit their children and the generations to follow. Your people are just now beginning to hear the harmony of the universe and they will respond to it." Gabe said with a look of relief on his face.

"What is the harmony of the universe?" I asked, forgetting my fears for a moment.

"The entire universe is one single connection. It has a single goal: to create itself! There is a sound it makes as it creates. It's a sound founded in harmony. Some of us refer to it as "the symphony." When there is dissonance anywhere, we are able to hear it and take steps to correct it. We ourselves are part of this great symphony that we live in. Your people have not heard that sound for thousands of years, but they will soon. Things are changing. This evil one wants to make sure this doesn't happen," Gabe explained.

"How do we fit into this drama Gabe? I asked with a skeptical look on my face. "What part are we supposed to play? How does a guy like me and his little girl fit into your cosmic plan?" I asked showing Gabe some contempt for what we were facing.

"Doug, you play a very important part in the whole plan. As you already know, we have been using you to channel new ideas, concepts, and formulas into human consciousness. We have worked for centuries to help move your race forward as a civilization. Our efforts have helped to grow the level of social consciousness to greater and greater heights. Unfortunately, in

147

the process, what we have learned is this growth produces bigger and bigger tragedies as well.

Every now and then a human monster is born…. someone with no conscious at all! These people are completely consumed with power and totally self-absorbed. They create social movements and gather power to themselves in an attempt to dominate the entire planet. The result is always the same… there is great suffering and many deaths." Gabe explained.

"These people are emotional vampires! They suck life from everyone around them, having no life of their own," Gabe said with a contemptuous look on his face.

"As the people around the world begin to wake up they will need guidance, instruction, and support. They will be moving in a direction that is unfamiliar to them. There will be a great need for spiritual teachers. I believe Ruth may be the one that becomes their spiritual leader someday. Everything I've come to know about her tells me she is a very strong person and a good person. She is an old soul and will learn quickly. She already understands that learning is important and she has a healthy curiosity about everything around her. Ruth is very strongly connected to the universe around her….to the one!" Gabe said as if he was seeing her future.

"She is a new element in this unfolding drama of humankind. She is so very young and may be in danger. You must protect her Doug. You must teach her what she needs to know and make her strong. She must learn to listen to her instincts and choose her own way in life. One day we may all be counting on her knowledge and strength to turn the tide of this battle we fight," Gabe said.

"This evil one we are speaking of has returned to this world. He is a dark lord from another place, another time. Actually for him, there is no time. His powers allow him to assume many forms. He is smoke or air. He can appear as water or rain. He can appear in any form he chooses, or, he can simply be present with no form at all!"

Gabe had lost me. I didn't really understand the meaning of his words. I didn't know why he was telling me these things. I could only think about my daughter's safety and how I was going to get her back home and how I was going to get myself back home. My family was never part of this bargain. In fact, I was never part of this bargain! I'm sorry I ever got mixed up with these guys. I'm sorry I ever went to Emma's and met Jim. I'm sorry I ever had lunch with Dr. Frankenstein!

How stupid of me to think that sooner or later my family wouldn't be affected by this crazy stuff, wouldn't be somehow involved in this stuff. My only thought now was to get Ruth out of here, to get her home with her mother and brothers, and to be done with this whole thing.

Gabe must have been tuned into my frequency. He sensed my anxiety. We both just sat there for the longest time staring at each other…then, staring off into space. I wondered what would happen next. I was no help at all. I couldn't think of anything except grabbing my daughter and going home as soon as possible, but I never know how to go home. That's Gabe's department. He always initiated the end of our meetings and orchestrated my return to Emma's and helped me find my way home. I had to wait for Gabe to get me and my daughter out of here. Eventually Gabe broke the silence.

"I know you would like to go home right now. You'd like to take Ruth and go back home to the rest of your family, but Doug, we have work to do now. Here in this place, in this sacred and holy place, I need to teach you many of the things you will need to know that will help you. There is a knowledge of things I can give you that will help protect you and your family and especially Ruth. But we must do this work now. Do I have your attention? Can we get started?" Gabe asked staring at me with deep intention.

I was suddenly startled and a little frightened to see the intense look on Gabe's face being directed at me. As much time as I've spent with Gabe, every now and then his size frightened me. This was one of those times. The look on Gabe's face told me I'd better speak up now.

"Yes. Yes Gabe. We can get started whenever you want," I said, realizing I was experiencing the fear of him. He smiled at me and instantly all my fear dissolved.

"Good! Let's start by getting something to eat," he said. We all got up and walked into another room filled with an assortment of food stuffs. The room looked like a veritable banquet hall.

Ruth seemed to be taking all this in as if it was part of her every day routine. We sat down at the table and started eating as many different items as we could sample.

"What's this daddy?" she'd say, handing me a small apple-looking fruit.

"I'm not sure baby," I said back to her after taking a bite. It sort of looked like an apple, but it had a taste and texture of a strawberry. There were cakes and pastries that had a texture like sourdough bread, but very sweet. All of the food was different and indescribable. It was delightful and wonderful and otherworldly. Ruth seemed to enjoy everything.

I watched intently as Ruth sampled everything they put in front of her. The people serving us were not all human-looking. There were creatures I had never seen, beings not of this earth. Ruth immediately accepted them as part of her normal. Occasionally she would ask Gabe who that was or why they didn't look like us. Gabe was always patient and offered her a simple yet thorough explanation about each of the beings serving us. Throughout the entire evening I watched Ruth interact with Gabe and the other aliens. She seemed at ease, almost at home with all of them. My heart was moved with a faint hope that our world was moving in the right direction.

It struck me as odd that I felt comfortable around them as well. I hadn't noticed before always being absorbed with Gabe's presence. I became aware of how unaware of these other creatures I had been before. Now though, with Ruth here, I was much more aware of all of them. Where did they come from? It was obvious they were not all from the same world, but why were they all here? Why did they all work for Gabe? The whole scene was wrapped in an enchanting mist with Ruth as the star attraction. I was spellbound watching her interact with all the creatures around us and especially with Gabe. It was as if we'd gone to a family reunion or something.

While Ruth and Gabe were enjoying their time together, I was being consumed by a fear of an unknown enemy from the inside out. Ruth ate her fill of everything while Gabe and I watched. We laughed and talked and watched the variety of dancers and singers that popped in and out of the evening as we dined. Finally, it was time for bed. Gabe took Ruth and me to a very warm comfortable room and told us he would come for us in the morning. As soon as our heads hit the pillows, we were both out like a light.

"THE HIGHER PLANES OF EXISTENCE"

Chapter 11

The first thing I noticed when I opened my eyes was the light streaming in from the small window at the end of the room. There were brilliant single strands of sunlight flowing in and cascading across the stone floor. Slowly and quietly I got out of bed and walked to the window. Peering out into the brilliant light my heart was seized with a moment of inspiration to see the ancient scene of dawn at Machu Picchu. It was a spiritually moving experience to watch the sunlight creep up the walls and mountainsides ever so slowly. As much as I could see of the place, it was spectacular! Each building, each sculpture, each part of the city came to life as the sun's rays lit it up. The entire world illuminated in stages. My eyes drank in the spectacular wonderment of the scene of light and shadows playing out in front of me. I quietly realized that we must be just inside one of the cliffs overlooking the site. It felt as if my soul was drinking it all in like an old friend from an ancient past. Our room was filling up with more and more sunlight. The day was coming quickly and my little girl would be waking soon.

Just then the door opened and Gabe walked in.

"I see you're awake," he said. Gabe and I looked over at Ruth still sleeping in her bed.

"Why don't you shower and we can meet a little later," Gabe said. I agreed and he left.

Ruth continued sleeping while I slipped into the bathroom and showered. She was still fast asleep when I returned from the shower. I knew she'd be okay if I left her for a bit. I knew there were beings in this place that would make sure she was okay.

I found Gabe waiting down the hall from my room.

"Hi Gabe," I said as I approached him.

"Doug. We have a busy day ahead of us. I suggest you get Ruth up and join me in the hall for some breakfast and we can talk a while," he said with a big smile on his face.

"Okay. I'll get her up and join you shortly," I said.

I went back to my room and Ruth was already stirring. She wasn't alone. One of the beings was there with her. It's hard to tell, but she seemed female with her patient and nurturing manner. She was not very tall, but light radiated from her as she was helping Ruth out of bed.

"Hi daddy," Ruth said when she saw me entering the room. "This is Emily. She's my friend," Ruth said introducing me to her new friend. Emily looked at me and smiled.

"You have a lovely daughter Doug. She is a very beautiful little girl," Emily said as she helped Ruth to get dressed. Her voice was heavenly. Emily had the most calming and purposeful manner about her. Whatever she was doing at any given moment was performed with a patient purposefulness. In this moment my eyes were opened to the profound meaning associated with simple acts of kindness offered to another without cost or thought of reward.

We caught up to Gabe in what appeared to be the main dining hall. We sat down at the table and immediately food was brought in and fresh coffee and juice. We all ate a hearty and delicious meal. During the meal Gabe began describing the day ahead of us.

"Today I need to give you a history lesson. It will be necessary for you to understand that the earth is not alone in the cosmos and that there are forces at work on earth that have their origins in other places and from another time," Gabe said.

"The being we've been talking about has a name. His name is Levant. Here on earth, he is considered a mythical being, but he is, in fact, quite real. He came here from the Kebraran system. The kebraranians believed him to be a godlike creature. He was alive and active before the Kebraranians were around. He came to them when they were just beginning to develop their civilization. He helped them to grow stronger, but not without a price. Levant carved them out from the unity of the universe and separated them from other species. They became self-aware and self-absorbed. They set up governments and armies and set goals of conquest,' Gabe explained.

"Their self-centered arrogance only served to strengthen their culture of greed and power until they needed a strong military to control them and maintain peace. Levant helped them with this last piece of the puzzle. He is a master at growing new leaders and generals for conflict. It's what he wants. It's how he eventually gets what he wants. What he wants is allegiance to his goals, to his power… to his being. He considers himself to be a god among creatures and he creates conflict and helps others in order to enslave them. His purpose on earth is to enslave the entire world population to bend their will to his needs. And it's happening. It's been happening for a few centuries now, degree by degree," Gabe said taking a breath. He'd been talking for quite a while.

We sat there for a few minutes not talking. I needed to absorb the conversation and subtle meanings. I had gathered some questions as he'd been talking.

"This Levant guy, how will we know him? What do we do if we meet him? Do we report him to you? I don't even know how to contact you Gabe!" I said realizing for the first time that I had no means of contacting him.

"Things are changing now Doug. Before you leave I will tell you how you can contact me. This is now the time when we will need to work more closely. Up until this moment it's been acceptable for us to contact you when we needed to talk, but now there needs to be two-way communications," Gabe said.

"Will Levant try and contact me? Is he trying to get to Ruth? Does he know about us? What do I need to do to protect my family?" I asked, now needing answers to my questions.

It was all too clear to me that Ruth and I were not much more than pawns in this celestial game of warfare that had taken place everywhere in the universe. Now his war had come to our world and to my family. We were reluctant soldiers in this war, this thing that is happening in our world. Our worst nightmare happens when our children are called upon to participate in war. I had come to the very end of myself in this waking nightmare. My four-year old little girl was a soldier!

"Yes. Most certainly he will try and make contact with you. He will work to gain your confidence and persuade you to join him and his organization," Gabe explained.

"How will I be able to recognize him?" I asked.

"You won't! You will most likely not know him or recognize him, at least not at first. But there are ways to learn someone's true intentions. Character will always reveals itself over time. Pay attention to the details," Gabe said. "He will undoubtedly try to determine how far you are into the program."

"What does that mean? How far am I into the program Gabe?" I asked.

"You are well into the program Doug. Actually you are totally in the program. You are now almost one of us. You are now second generation into the program with Ruth involved," Gabe said looking at me expecting a reaction.

I didn't give him any reaction. I already knew I was totally in the program. I knew it for sure when I was reviewing the scrolls at the Sphinx. I knew then that somehow my life, my part in living was now connected to these people, for better or for worse. I had tried to convince myself that none of this was true and not really happening. Now with Ruth here I see that this whole effort involves everyone. It involves the whole world and I also know I can't run away from my part. Most of us don't believe we have a real part to play, but we all do. I know if I quit now, it won't change anything. It won't change my life except to make it worse. I know that we are all connected on this planet and either we work together for a common good or we don't. Gabe's comments didn't affect me in the least. I knew my level of dedication to the program has gone up significantly now that Ruth was involved. I would learn everything I could learn about them, about their program, and about Levant.

"I know Gabe," I said, looking at him with a new level of confidence and commitment. "I'll do whatever needs to be done to protect my daughter and to help the cause…to help you in your work."

Gabe said, "We need to talk about Levant. I need to tell you his story."

"I'm all ears Gabe. Tell me what I need to know," I said, giving him my full attention.

I noticed Ruth sitting there with us absorbing all we were saying. She never spoke, but only looked at Gabe and then at me. I could tell she was taking in our every word and somehow I knew she would make sense of it someday. She sat there silently as Gabe prepared himself for what appeared to be a long story.

"There was a time on earth when mankind was very young. Your species had recently come out from the jungle and savannas and began to settle in what would become cities. They gathered themselves together in communities and began to farm the lands. It was during this time that Levant made an appearance in Persia. He was one of the antagonists of Zoroastrianism. He fostered a belief in many gods and prayed on the fears of the people that inhabited those lands. He presented himself as an angel of light. Such are his ways. He is a master at coaxing people into being selfish and arrogant. He always provided the means for people to dominate those around them. Levant used religion as a means to creating myth, which eventually, turns into believable history. The result is a mindless faith in him and the power he offers. Of course, Zoroastrianism went on to earn a valid place in the thoughts of humankind, but Levant never stopped trying to deceive them," Gabe explained.

"There were many other events in your history that he was involved in, but we won't discuss them now. Let's just say that

159

Levant has been defeated many times in your world. When that happens- he leaves for a while. He's been gone a very long time, but his minions work ceaselessly to bring the world under his control. He left behind an army of powerful beings that intermingle with humans, but they are not human. It is these that we work against. It is his army of the lost that work to foil our plans. Somehow, we always manage to get another step up on them and stay ahead of their foul plans. We are all tireless workers in this struggle between good and evil. We believe that good must win in the end," Gabe said, looking at me.

"This is a war for the future of humankind Doug. We can help, but humankind must fight the battle. That's how it has been presented to us. That's how it must play out. We can help, but we cannot fight this battle for you," he said almost pleading with me.

Levant spent centuries cultivating a deep-rooted sense of patriotism, dividing people by culture, by religion, by species, and by nationality. And it works! He's managed to convince the people of earth that they are not all the same. He teaches them to focus on their differences and then exploits those differences. He introduces ideas of ethnic and cultural superiority among those who listen to him. Every tribe, every nation, every culture on earth has some elements of superiority in it. Levant exploits that single emotion, that solitary idea to enslave his followers. They learn war and before they know it, they've started a campaign they must continue until there is a winner. He' helped usher in the age of scientific materialism!" Gabe paused here.

"Have you understood me to say that Levant is a divider of peoples?" Gabe asked.

"Yes," I answered. His question caught me off guard.

160

"Can you now begin to see some of the failings of your modern scientific method?" he asked.

"I'm not sure I understand the question Gabe," I replied.

"Doug, the very basis of scientific materialism is to divide things into smaller and smaller bits of realty! Then your scientists study those time bits and whatever they observe, they decide that it is real! It's only one way of looking at things. They will better serve your race when they begin to develop more holistic methods of examination. There is much more to life and reality than quarks and neutrinos, even Higgs Bosons!" Gabe said with a smile.

"You see Doug, Levant fully understands a simple truth about the people of your world: we are all connected! Each one of us is a small critical part of a much larger whole being. We are life! All life is sacred and forged to serve its own purpose in the cosmos. These spiritual principles have been practiced from the beginning in your world, but they are fragile. They can be easily ignored or worse, forgotten!"

"The duality of all things exists in only one place-it exists in our minds! Our mind is the one place where all the rules of the universe can be changed, can be ignored, and rewritten. It is the mind that creates its own isolation, its own prison, and its own hell! Once that happens, it becomes difficult to change direction. It becomes difficult to change your mind about things. Levant understands this and he uses ideas and emotions to forge whole species into following him," Gabe said.

"The cycle of life and death is based on the very strong experience of living in a singular physical body. The temptations of living in the flesh are very, very strong. It is easily corruptible,

161

but in order for this to happen, you must ignore the other parts of the creature. You do this by destroying the spirit and then corrupting the heart. Once this is accomplished, the creature can be turned to any evil purpose," Gabe said.

I listened to Gabe explain these things and realized I hadn't considered any of the issues he was speaking about. I never believed there was a spiritual life or any spiritual component of being human. It always felt like bullshit to me until my children were born, until I realized how much I loved Mary. Only then could I begin to understand the central importance of belonging to a family and how much that means to us. My wife and my children are the most important things in my life. Everything else runs a very distant second.

Family is the most important ingredient in the life we live. It is the focal point of our existence no matter what position you choose. What he was saying began to make sense to me in a way I had never envisioned. My spiritual side always felt more like a collage of strange feelings. It never felt real to me, but now, listening to Gabe, I began to see and feel the tangible side of spirituality and why people believe.

Suddenly I realized the obvious….all the pieces fell into place and I instantly began to understand the spiritual component of my own being. There is it! It had always been there, waiting silently for me to become aware of myself. My whole life I had been a doer. I never thought of myself as simply being present in a place and doing nothing. There was my spirit never judging me, never interfering in my life, and never insisting on its own way. There was a moment of integration where I felt myself becoming whole, becoming a complete person. Now so many other aspects of my life began to make sense, began to matter to me. Then it occurred to me that I was in the middle of a spiritual awakening! I had been asleep before! How could I have lived so long and not seen everything I was now seeing? How is that possible?

"This war is not a conventional war. It's not really a physical war, is it?" I asked.

"Well, yes, Doug. It's actually both. On the surface, it will be a physical war. It has been a spiritual war in terms of human emotions and human weakness. As we go on, it could become more physical with respect to a physical invasion of the Earth. This is a possibility. But this is also a very spiritual war in that there are opposing energies, spiritual energies that are at work at a level not seen by the human eye. We have been training you, setting the foundation in you for this spiritual warfare. Ruth has already surpassed you on a spiritual level. She is young and her soul and heart are open to the holistic food we offer. Your heart and mind have been fairly closed to such options yet you are now changing and beginning to open up. I always knew you would get to this point in your training," Gabe said.

"The entire universe is nothing more than expressed potential. It is form from the formless. That which cannot be seen supports that which can be seen. There is an underlying force that permeates everything that is, even that which cannot be seen." Gabe said. What we've come to understand is that you humans have a capacity to affect that formless energy. In the entire universe there are no other creatures that have this power. It's been difficult for us knowing what you as a species are capable of, and not being able to teach you how to harness this ability. The human race has always been engulfed in the mundane aspects of living their lives and all the social values and choices that come with it." Gabe explained.

Just then, Ruth climbed into my lab. She looked at Gabe and said, "Daddy, I want to go home now."

"We'll go shortly baby. Gabe and I are talking now, but soon we'll go home."

"But I want to go now Daddy. I miss mommy!" she said looking very sad.

"Gabe, we have to go. How do we do that? I need to get my little girl home."

"It is time for you both to go. I've kept you too long already. But you can't go together. Don't worry Doug. We'll take Ruth to another room and she will wake up in her own bedroom. The transportation for small children is different than for adults. We will get you back to the restaurant very soon as well," Gabe said.

With that, I hugged Ruth and said, "Honey, you need to go with Gabe now. He's going to take you home to mommy."

"I want to go with you daddy," she said, pleading with me.

"I can't go now honey, but I'll be home very soon." I picked Ruth up and gave her a big kiss and a hug and put her back down. "Now go with Gabe now and tell mommy I'll be home soon."

Gabe and Ruth disappeared through the door. This was all so strange and stressful. Within five minutes, Gabe was back in the room. "She's home already. She's sleeping in her bed just as we found her. With a little luck, she will think this was all a dream," Gabe explained.

"You mean she won't remember this?" I asked.

"Well, she may remember it, but it will be a little fuzzy for her," Gabe explained. "Now we need to get you back to the restaurant and your friend Bob. We will be contacting you very soon Doug. If you need to contact us, all you need to do is to turn on your television to channel 777 and wait. We monitor that frequency and when someone tunes into it, we pick up the signal very quickly. Once we do, we can make arrangements to transport you to our location."

"We'll need another session so we can make plans to help you and Ruth to prepare for your meeting with Levant. He will come to you at some point. We need to make sure you both have the tools you'll need to protect yourselves and also to stay one step ahead of him. You and Ruth are not the front line in our war with Levant, but he has taken an interest in you. We want to make sure you both are protected."

"Let me know when you want to meet again. I have only one request: please let's not do it at Emma's!" I asked. "Next time we meet, it will be much easier Doug," Gabe promised.

Just then Micah appeared in the doorway and said, "Ready to go Doug?"

"I'm ready Micah," I said. Gabe reached out and hugged me.

"You take care of yourself and your little girl. We will be very close Doug, so do not worry," Gabe said, giving me a look of complete trust.

Micah and I walked down a hallway and into a room. Soon the room turned transparent and we were up in the air and on our way back to Emma's. I walked out of the bathroom and back into Denny's just in time to see Bob take a bite out of his sandwich. It was a bit disconcerting and dizzying to pop in and out of time. This time it didn't seem as bad.

"There you are buddy! Your foods getting cold," Bob said with half a mouthful of food.

We finished our lunch and talked about the upcoming BBQ with Walter and Jim. Bob seemed satisfied with the updates I shared with him. We wrapped up our business and agreed to stay in touch every day through the end of the project.

I found my car and pulled out onto the freeway heading for home. How many more times will this happen to me? How is this all going to end? My mind was abuzz with a million new questions. Every drive home from Emma's was the same for me. I always struggled to assimilate the entire experience before I pull into my driveway. I can't take this stuff home with me. I just can't. As usual, the closer I got to home, the more relaxed I felt and my recent adventure became more dreamlike. When I finally pulled into my driveway, Mary was out the front door before I even turned the motor off!

"Doug, thank God your home! It's Ruth again. We've got to talk. I don't know what to think or what to do anymore!" she said with tears in her eyes.

My heart was racing seeing Mary in such a condition. What had happened while I was gone? I suddenly felt a wave of fatigue sweep over me. I don't know how many more twists and turns my life can take before the wheels come off. We went inside as I took several deep breaths to prepare myself for whatever was upsetting my wife.

"It's Ruth! When she woke up from her nap today she told me she had been with you and your friends again," Mary said with a wild look in her eyes.

"I'm sorry honey. Poor baby! I'm sorry Ruthie is having these problems. I feel bad. I feel like it's my entire fault," I said feeling ashamed of the whole affair.

"Ruth told me today that she had been with you and Gabe, which was bad enough, but, she told me you were in Machu Picchu! How does our baby girl even know that name?" Mary said stunned and shocked at her own words.

"Let me see if I can explain this," I said as we both sat on the couch.

"HUMAN SOCIAL SUPRANETICS"

Chapter 12

I could see from the tension in Mary's face that she'd had a bad day and was upset. I took a deep breath and began: "When I met Bob for lunch today, I made another side trip to Emma's Café. It seemed like I was gone for a very long time, but as usual, when I got back to real time, only a few minutes had gone by. This time was very different than all the other times I've met with Gabe and Micah. This time Ruth was there!" I blurted out. Mary just stared at me, seeming to calculate what my words might mean. I didn't say anything, not knowing what to say next.

"Ruth was with you? The aliens took Ruth? She wasn't dreaming? She was actually there with you? How? Why?" Mary asked.

"Doug, I thought these were bad dreams and what I'm hearing is that these things are actually happening! And Ruth is involved in these activities!" Mary said with a concerned look on her face.

"I'm not sure of anything anymore Mary. Gabe said that Ruth has an extraordinary power, but did not tell me what it was. He said she is the one they've been looking for, not me. Gabe said he thought it was me, but when Ruth was born, he could tell that she would be the one to help them," I said, not knowing what else to say.

"Help them how? What do they want Ruth to do?" Mary said.

"Gabe said there could be some trouble coming and that he and his kind would be watching us both very closely. He said he'd contact me soon for some training he said I needed to learn." I added.

"What kind of trouble? What kind of training?" Mary asked.

"I don't know. He said it would help to keep us all safe from whatever trouble they are expecting. Gabe said there is a dark force at work in the world and somehow, Ruth and I can play a part is helping to stop it. That's all he told me this time. He said he'd contact me soon."

Mary just looked at me. She seemed to be at a loss for words. At one point, she started to speak, but then didn't say anything. She had heard and understood as much as there was to understand at this point. It had been a long day for all of us, so we had a quick dinner and went to bed.

The next few weeks seemed to fly by, but no word from Gabe. As usual, it only takes a few days back in my real world routine for my alien adventures to start wearing off. It's happened several times during long periods with no contact. After enough time passes, my alien abductions seem more like bad dreams. I'm not sure if it has something to do with time travel or being out of time, but after I've been back for a while, the memories take on a more dreamlike quality. Their sense of urgency fades and my memories become part of a distant reality.

It's not that I've forgotten anything from my many trips. It's more like they exist inside me as a separate and unbelievable reality. They are smaller and less bright than my daily routine. This time though, I had the distinct feeling that both realities were moving toward one another. It was a feeling I couldn't shake, so I tried not to think about it too much.

I started for the bedroom and decided to use the bathroom in the hall so I wouldn't wake Mary when I went to bed. As I closed the door to the bathroom I got a strange feeling and realized immediately I was not alone!

"Micah! What are you doing in my bathroom?" I blurted out. Micah just smiled and in an instant we were high above my house. "I hope we didn't wake my wife," I said realizing how loud I must have been when I spoke Micah's name.

"Not to worry Doug. We have experience with this kind of transfer and your bathroom was sound-proofed, so nobody heard anything, "Micah explained.

"Where are we going this time?" I asked.

"Vegas," Micah answered.

"Vegas!" I yelled. What's in Vegas?" I asked.

"That's where Gabe said to bring you," Micah explained. Within minutes we were over Las Vegas. The spacecraft flew over the city and somewhere just outside Vegas we descended underground. I don't know how far down we went, but when the door opened I stepped out into a now familiar tropical environment, filled with strange scenes and even stranger creatures. It was like this whole network of bases was connected by some kind of a jungle where you go down this path and pop out here or go down that path and pop out somewhere else.

Micah led me down a path and we came to a clearing to a small hut. Gabe was inside waiting for us.

"Doug! Good to see you again," Gabe said.

"Hi Gabe," I replied.

"Doug, we don't have much time, so let's get to work. Levant is getting close to you. If you haven't been contacted yet, you will be very soon. You need to be aware of any new people coming into your life," Gabe said.

"Gabe. My daughter had a bad dream just a while ago. In fact, just before I came here my wife was telling me that Ruth woke up from her nap today screaming "they're coming!" I explained.

"Then she is already aware of what we know. She is an amazing little girl. It's as if she can see thing before they happen. She has a gift Doug and you need to listen to her when she tells you of her concerns." Gabe said with a piercing look of concern on his face.

"I understand Gabe. I will keep an eye out for anyone hanging around my house." I said.

"The reason we brought you here Doug is to train you how to respond when Levant makes his move. We are not exactly sure how he will approach you or how he intends to use you and Ruth, but we want you to be ready when it happens," Gabe said. "If Levant contacts you and you are able to positively identify him, you need to do the following things: you must clear your mind and body of all thoughts and feelings. You must be completely empty inside. We've been practicing this exercise, so you know what I'm speaking of. Secondly, when your interior space is clear and the waters of your soul are calm like a mirror, simply ask the universe for protection from all harm," Gabe said.

"What!" I yelled. "Gabe, what the hell are you trying to tell me? Don't you have some kind of a weapon or some special devise I can have that will disable him or stop him?" I yelled.

"Doug, there are many things you do not understand. The people in the world have long forgotten the power of utterance and the sacred power of the spoken word. When you speak the words I have given you, you initiate an immediate response from the universe that will create power enough to serve your purpose," Gabe explained.

"How is that possible?" I asked exasperated. "That sounds like something my priest would tell me. You guys are beyond all that stuff, aren't you?" I asked, expecting a better answer than what I was hearing.

"Well Doug. You need to trust us. We've been at this business for a long time. I'm telling you these spoken words will offer you protection. They will buy you time and they will give us a chance to move in and do what we can to win the day. That's how we've worked for a very long time. You humans mostly fail to recognize the true power and effect your mind has on the universe. You still don't believe the universe will serve your needs. You'll just need to trust us on this one," Gabe said with a big smile.

"One more thing you need to know. If you need to contact us you need to turn on your television set and turn it to channel 777. Then wait for us. We always monitor channel 777 and we'll pick up your signal," Gabe instructed.

Somehow I believed him. His advice sounded crazy and naïve, but his smile and calm confidence told me that he knew what he was doing.

"Okay Gabe. I trust you on this," I said and thinking I had little other choice in this matter.

"Good. Now let's get you back so you can get some sleep," Gabe said. With that, Micah appeared and I was soon back in my bathroom and alone. I went to bed, but could not sleep. I kept thinking about the words Gabe told and every time I turned over, I could see my wife sleeping quietly next to me.

"DIVINE HYBRID"

175

Chapter 13

Mary had done a great job preparing everything for the BBQ. We were the first to arrive at the local park and set up the table and BBQ. We had just about finished when Bob and his family arrived. A few minutes later Mr. Harrison arrived with a friend.

"Hi Doug, hi Mary," Bob said as he and his family walked up.

"Hey Bob. Glad you guys could make it," I yelled back. I gave Bob a hug and then hugged his wife Betty.

"Hi Doug," Betty said.

"Hi Betty," I said.

"Hi Mary," Betty yelled and walked over to where Mary was sorting out the lunch items. Just then Mr. Harrison walked up with his friend and I was stunned at who was with him. A bolt of lightning shot through me and my knees felt weak!

"Mr. Harrison, I mean Walter. How are you?" I said, looking at his friend. I couldn't believe my eyes. Was I seeing things? What did this mean?

"Hi Doug, hey, I brought a friend. I hope you don't mine. This is my friend Jim," he said, turning to Jim. It was Jim! It was Dr. Frankenstein at my barbeque! What was he doing here? I took a moment and a breath to calm down and said:

"Hi Jim. It's a pleasure to meet you," I said a bit cautiously wondering what Jim would say. I was curious how he was playing this.

"Hi Doug, it's a pleasure to meet you. I've heard a lot about you," he said shaking my hand and smiling with a piercing look.

"How do you know Mr. Harrison, I mean, Walter? How do you know him?" I asked, feeling myself starting to sweat. I wasn't sure what was going on between us. We both knew we knew each other, but neither of us made a move to acknowledge that fact. Jim had something up his sleeve. For whatever reason Jim didn't want Walter or Bob to know that he knew me from long ago. I decided to keep my mouth shut and let Jim make the first move.

"Oh, we've been friends for a long time, but now we're actually working together," Jim said. Bob walked up and joined the conversation.

"Hi Walter, hi Jim! Glad you guys could make it. Looks like we're going to enjoy quite a spread today! Doug and Mary have gone all out on the food," Bob said.

My mind was reeling. How are these guys connected? Why was Jim here? How long had he been friends with Walter? Was Jim Levant? How could he be? Was Walter Levant? That's it! This is too strange to not mean something. How could Walter be Levant? He was too nice! Besides, Jim worked for Gabe. Why would Jim get involved with the enemy? It didn't make any sense. Maybe I was overreacting. Mary and Betty were busy putting things out and making drinks for everyone. I started the BBQ, grabbed a beer, as the guys gathered around the BBQ.

"So Jim, what do you do with the company?" I asked. Walter, Jim, and Bob had all grabbed a beer and it looked like we were settling into a gabfest and BBQ session.

"Well I'm a kind of technical advisor, you might say. I work with Bob here on his projects and I also report to Walter and help him with some of his business," Jim replied, looking at me with a slight smile.

"So Doug, how are you and Rick coming along with your first deliverables? Ready for the next step?" Jim asked.

"Yes. We're moving along and looking forward to the lab testing next week," I responded.

"Look at those kids play!" Walter exclaimed. We all looked over at the kids. They were kicking around a ball and making up some kind of game that looked to be a cross between soccer and dodge ball.

"Look at your daughter Doug! She seems to be holding her own against the boys," Walter added.

"Yes, Ruth is quite capable of dishing it out and dealing with the consequences as well. She's a very resourceful little girl." I said.

"Makes me wish I had had children of my own," Walter added.

Walter and Bob wandered over to where the women were laying out the table and setting up for lunch. It gave me an opportunity to speak with Jim alone.

"Jim, it's been a long time since I've seen you. How did you get hooked up with Walter?" I asked.

"Well, it's a long story. After I moved out of town I went back to Riverton for a while, but I stopped being contacted by "the crew". After a year or so, I moved down south and went to work at the company that Walter ended up buying. I had a slight advantage over most of the other geeks in the place due to my experience with "you know who", so I rose to the top fairly quickly. When Walter came on board he cleaned house, but he kept me. Then a while back he hired Bob," Jim explained.

"So you and Walter aren't involved with "them at all?" I asked.

"No! He doesn't know them and I'm out of the program. Walter's company is a fascinating place to work. Many of his programmers are geniuses at what they do. He's merged them into teams with scientists and visionaries who worked together to dream up this latest project. It's simply breath-taking in its scope! I mean when we pull this off, our companies will own the Internet, the future of robotics, and genomics! Have you considered the implications of our success Doug?" he asked.

"Well, I think it's a great opportunity for both companies and the project certainly has huge benefits for all humankind, but we do have some formidable challenges ahead of us," I offered. "Consider the chip implant and the millions of neural connectors that need to happen to integrate the unit with the biological host. The biological and technical challenges are enormous!" I explained.

Neither of us spoke for a few minutes giving me time to ponder the meaning of what I knew or suspected. The significance of some of my earlier work came into focus and I began to realize the importance of some of my own personal theories I hadn't shared with my boss or my company. One in particular, work I had done studying the physical properties of synapses; measuring them, evaluating how they traveled through the neural network, and how they began and ended their trip. What had fascinated me were the subtle chemical reactions required to make it all work.

Brain chemistry was much more complicated than understanding the neural network as a whole. The concepts were straight forward, but the underlying chemical functions were much less obvious. I had come to understand much more than I had shared. I'm not sure if I had had received help with these experiments from Gabe and his crew. It was possible, but I didn't know for sure. Maybe at some point in the past Gabe had downloaded some extraordinary information into my brain and now it was coming out in a meaningful way. The question I always asked myself was: What were they teaching me? How were they teaching me? Why were they teaching me? All I knew for sure was my conscious experiences with them. What was happening to me on an unconscious level? I didn't know!

"How's the food coming along Doug?" Walter asked. I had drifted into a daydream and hadn't noticed his approach.

"Almost done Walter," I replied, looking at him and then at Jim.

"Say Walter, how long have you and Jim and Bob been working on this project together?" I asked. The words escaped my mouth before I could calculate the implications.

Walter looked at Jim and then back at me, "Oh, probably a couple of years, although we were all working on parts of the program separately. It wasn't until a couple of years ago at a brain storming meeting that the concept came together and the project was formed," Walter explained.

"Doug, here's the thing; my vision for us, for all of us, is that we can one day harness the collective knowledge of humanity through the use of quantum computers. If we can focus that knowledge into a single thinking unit where the true potential of the knowledge can be extracted, I believe that "Eve" and "NOAH" will allow humankind to make the next evolutionary step. I believe that NOAH and Eve will eventually become self-consciousness," Walter shared.

"Eve? Who's Eve? I asked.

"Oh, I'm sorry! Eve is the name we've given to the biological host. While NOAH is the name for the quantum computer, or more correctly, the software programs, Eve is the biological counterpart. We thought it was kind of catchy to name the biological host after our mythical mother. I like biblical stuff, Doug," Walter explained. "Do you like it?" he asked with a big smile.

"Yeah, it's really cool!" I replied.

"That is our ultimate goal, but in the meantime, there are millions of practical applications Eve can perform for companies, countries, and organizations around the world. Eve will be a technical and biological hybrid that will operate every bit as a human can by using her hands, eyes, ears, nose, sense of touch, and smell. She'll be able to interact with us and at the same time...in a human way. She will be in constant communication with the host computer. She will have nearly unlimited computing power plus a massive source of incoming information from the entire Internet! There has never been such an opportunity in history for a single capable host to absorb such a large volume of information in real time," he shared.

"How will NOAH and Eve co-exist together in the same 'brain' so to speak? How will they work together?" I asked, trying to piece the whole scene together.

"Honestly we're not sure exactly how it will work. We won't know until we complete our work and begin field testing her and measuring her cognitive skills. One of the critical steps in the process will be to measure the way NOAH and Eve affect each other and the direction their neural plasticity dynamic will guide them. It's an unknown factor Doug! Over time we expect that NOAH will begin utilizing the mind map algorithms at his disposal. That will be another critical point in the project," he continued.

"Eve will become a kind of oracle for humanity. Ask her a question and she will give you the answer almost instantly. She won't eliminate human researchers and scientists, but she's going to come very close!" Walter commented.

Bob had wandered over midway through Walter's discourse on Eve and the four of us stood there around the barbeque. He hadn't said anything, waiting for Walter to finish. Now that he had finished we all just stood there watching the food cook and pondering Walter's words. Each of us seemed to be lost in our own calculations of the significance of what we were doing as a team and I was wondering where this whole thing was going to end up.

"Food's ready," I said, breaking the spell. "Let's eat!" Everyone gathered at the table. Mary and Betty placed the children at one end and us men at the other. It seemed better that way. As we began to eat, Walter started speaking with the children.

"Do you boys play sports?" he asked.

"I play baseball," Justin answered.

"I play football," Doug junior replied.

"How about you Ruth? Do you play any sports or are you not ready for sports yet?" Walter asked.

Ruth looked directly at Walter, but didn't say a word. She then looked at me and then back at Walter, never speaking.

"Ruth, Mr. Harrison asked you a question. Aren't you going to answer him? Mary asked. Ruth didn't say a word. She looked down at her plate and pretended to ignore us.

"I'm sorry Mr. Harrison; sometimes Ruth can be shy around strangers," Mary explained. I wasn't sure what to make of Ruth's behavior, so I let it pass.

After lunch the kids all went back to playing. Mary and Betty sat near them and supervised the games. The men all moved back toward the barbeque for a quiet post lunch discussion. Bob started the conversation.

" Doug, are you guys going to be ready to go next week with the interface trials?" he asked.

"Yes, Rick has been working on that part and he said we're ready," I replied.

"Good! If next week's testing goes well, we can move on to establishing the biological parameters for integration of the computer chip into the organic tissue," Doug added.

Jim was obviously quiet. He and Walter had gotten quiet at lunch and now did not seem to be in the mood for further discussion. After a few minutes of awkward silence, Walter shared that he and Jim needed to leave. He said they had some other appointments to make and needed to get back to the plant by the end of the day. Bob and I thanked them for coming and bid them farewell. After they left, I asked Bob,

"Bob, how long have you known Jim?" I asked.

Bob gave me a questioning look, one that suggested he wasn't sure where this conversation would go.

"I met Jim about a month after I started at Galaxy. The company wasn't sure where they would assign me and Jim said he needed some help, so I ended up working with him on this project," Bob replied.

"Funny you ask that since Jim was one of the few people that didn't get the ax when Mr. Harrison took over the company. He and Mr. Harrison seemed to be quite a team when I came on board. I just assumed they'd been friends and colleagues for a long time," Bob said. "Working with Jim, I can tell you he's brilliant, but also a bit odd. He keeps to himself a lot, but every now and then, he acts a little strange," Bob shared.

"Explain." I asked.

"Well on a couple of occasions he's mentioned to me that he believes in aliens from outer space! He said he's actually seen them. I thought that was weird! What was really weird was he actually believes it happened to him," Bob said.

"Can you tell me anything about his relationship with Mr. Harrison?" I asked.

"Only that they seem to get along well and they work well together. Jim seems to understand what our boss wants from him and he works hard to deliver, just like I do," Bob said.

I didn't want to try and explain my previous relationship with Jim. It would be too messy and besides, I wasn't sure now exactly what was going on with this project. I started to smell something else happening here. I wasn't at all sure what it might be, but my gut was telling me there was more to this project than what I'd been told. Also, there was more to Mr. Harrison than what I've already learned. The fact that Jim had reappeared in my life and was connected to Mr. Harrison was too great a coincidence to ignore! Maybe this was what Gabe has been preparing me for.

"Only one more question for you Bob: Does your program have any other goal beyond marketing the services that Eve can provide?" I asked.

"Not sure I understand your question Doug," Bob replied.

"I mean, could Mr. Harrison have another use or purpose for NOAH and Eve? Are you aware of any other plans for NOAH and Eve?" I asked.

"No. None that I'm aware of Doug," Bob replied. "Why? What's going on with you? Why are you asking me such weird question?" Bob asked.

"I'm not sure Bob. There just seems to be some strange things going on and I needed to know where you stand in this deal," I replied.

**"THE SHATTERING OF HUMAN BONDS |
OBSIDIAN"**

Chapter 14

The next three weeks flew by. All the tests went as planned and we were ready to move into phase four. What we had learned so far is this: the chip implant was not being rejected and was functioning with a clear signal. Our preliminary testing on the synthetic axons and dendrite connections kept coming up with favorable results. We had proved that synthetic axons could and would positively interact with biological dendrite in a way that would produces synapses. There was little doubt that, given the proper host, we could move forward with the program. We would be successful! This project was going to work!

As we moved closer and closer to the deadline, I began having anxieties about the biology portion of the project. Our team had assembled a collection of living brain tissue, but would it work? Had we actually coaxed a living brain from stem cells? Is it possible for us to construct even portions of a human brain? Will they work? Can they function and learn? Will NOAH 'teach' Eve what she needs to know? How will Eve 'experience' life? These questions haunted me and woke me up in my sleep. *What are we doing here?*

I admired Walter for his humanitarian values. This whole project would be much easier if we had a human brain. It was out of the question! Our team was close to solving Walter's alternative solution for the project. If this worked, we'd all get a Nobel peace prize!

How will Eve 'feel' once she gains consciousness? How long will it take for her to become self-aware? What else would she learn? Will she be capable of making moral choices? Will she develop a sense of right and wrong? Will she eventually figure out how she came into being? Will she realize she is the only one of her kind? And if all this comes about, how will Eve react to her new found knowledge of herself? Would she begin to exhibit more human characteristics? Could she learn to be compassionate? Would she begin to 'feel' love or hate? What would be the extent of her human emotions?

I hadn't really considered any of these questions when we started. I had been more concerned with the technical aspects of the project. It's my job to do these things. Yes, Eve could and would be successful at becoming a one-stop Internet exchange, but what would she do with all that personal information? What could she do with it? What would others do with it? Eve would be the "fork in the road" for all humanity. She would be the first bio-machine that would have the mental capacity to create new operating programs with NOAH's help. She could write whatever code she chooses to write!

Suddenly, all my fears lined up in a pattern that made sense. All the pieces of the puzzle came together and showed me a picture of what might be, of what could be. Yes! Jim was part of this drama. He had been a part from very long ago if not from the very beginning. Walter was Levant! He was the evil one that Gabe has been talking about. It made sense to me now. Walter was going to use his quantum computer to create a human interface with it for the purpose of downloading material to human unconsciousness! Jim was helping him, but I don't think Jim would become the human host. No. Jim was a technical advisor only. He was only a co-conspirator in this deal.

It was all very clear now. Levant was going to use his quantum computer to download information into human unconsciousness that would help him to take control of humanity and the whole world. They would be defenseless against him. It would almost seem like it was their idea to be conquered, no not conquered, to be governed. Yes. Levant would encourage them to want bigger and stronger government and he would provide it of course. I had to make a game plan to stop Walter. I had to talk with Gabe!

As my life began to unravel before my eyes fate interjected another player into the game. The next day at work Rick called me into his office.

"Doug, we have a new prospective customer coming in tomorrow and I want you to sit in," Rick said.

"Rick, can we afford to take on any new customers at this time? This NOAH project is going to tax our whole team for the next several weeks if not months! I don't think it's a good idea," I said, wondering if Rick had lost his mind.

"Doug, it's a preliminary meeting. There may be no business there at all, but we at least need to see them. We can at least find out the nature of their project and their timeline. Maybe we can schedule them in after the NOAH project. Did you ever think about that?" Rick said, helping me realize why he was the CEO and I was only the head researcher.

"I didn't think of it that way Rick. I'm just wound up with this NOAH project and can't seem to think of anything else. You're right of course. It's business," I said a little sheepishly.

"Okay. Who's the customer? What are they looking for?" I asked.

"His name is Damien Hess. He's the CEO and President of Hessen Enterprises," Rick replied.

"What do they do and why do they need us?" I asked.

"Hessen Enterprises is basically a software company, but they are heavily invested with the Internet. There are several divisions in the company. They have a medical devices division and an electronics division. They manufacturer industrial robots and their software company create search engines for the Internet. I'm not exactly sure why they need us or what they want from us. I guess we'll both find out tomorrow at the meeting," Rick said.

"What time?" I asked.

"Ten A.M. right here in my office," Rick replied.

"Thanks boss. I'll see you at ten. Thanks for the talk," I said and walked out.

The next morning I was sitting in Rick's office when Mr. Hess and company arrived. I didn't like him the moment I saw him. He was barely five foot five inches tall and had an evil air about him. For a man with such short stature he exuded a huge physical presence that made the hair on the back of my neck stand up! He could have been one of the Nazis that got away, but he wasn't old enough. He would have been only a baby during the war. Still, his persona exuded an air of fanaticism. I could feel him!

He looked to be a no-nonsense type of businessman. He had short dark hair with touches of gray around his ears and a small bald spot on top. There was a small scar that started from the left side of his lip and went almost to the point of his chin. He had two other men with him. Both were much taller and sinister looking. They too looked like refugees from Hitler's Gestapo!

One of the men was six feet tall and was obviously very muscular. He had a mustache and a small scar next to his right eye. His hair was blond with a chiseled face. The other man was of average height, brown hair, and wore glasses. When he looked at you it was as if he was looking right through you.

"Mr. Hess! So nice to meet you in person," Rick said, extending a hand with a big smile.

"Mr. Flannigan. Thank you for seeing me." Mr. Hess replied, with a slight upturn at the corner of his mouth as if it hurt for him to smile. From his facial expressions it was apparent that Mr. Hess was bothered wasting his time visiting us. It may have been nothing and I could be wrong.

"These are my two associates. This is doctor Hammersfeld. His specialty is computer science. My other associate is doctor Arnstadt. Doctor Arnstadt is a neurosurgeon and neuroscientist. They both are working closely on our new project with me," Mr. Hess commented.

"This is my colleague and associate Doug Keller. Doug is our chief researcher here," Rick said.

"Mr. Keller. Pleased to meet you," Mr. Hess said, extending a cold impersonal hand toward me as if I wasn't worth the effort. He couldn't seem to manage a smile for me.

"My pleasure Mr. Hess," I replied, smiling a big smile and shaking his limp, lifeless hand.

"Well, please come in and let's have a seat at the conference table and see if my company can be of any help to you in your project," Rick said, gesturing us all toward his conference table. Once we were all seated, Mr. Hisses spoke:

"Mr.Flannigan, we chose your biotech company for two reasons: you have an award winning research department, and your genomics department is the best in the country. My colleagues and I have been working on a very ambitious project and we need an outside partner to perform some of the work for us. Since you've signed the non-disclosure agreement, I believe we can begin to discuss some of the aspects of the project. I'll let doctor Hammersfeld begin," he said

"For several years now, our team has been working on a revolutionary new product. This new product will allow Hessen Enterprises to create a new opportunity in the field of medicine. Our goal is to develop the technology to create a 'Post-human" division for the company. This new division will usher in a new age for humanity! We believe we have perfected the software and algorithms to a point where we are ready to begin testing on a biological interface. That's why we've come to your firm," Dr. Hammersfeld said.

"I believe that doctor Arnstadt has a few words to add to the good doctor's description," Mr. Hess said.

"The piece we need to complete our project is a human brain. If we can find the right brain and connect it to our machine, we believe we will achieve the breakthrough in artificial intelligence. Together with the machine, the bio-computer will have the ability to write code that is not possible today. There are still too many variables in the human brain that are not easily solved writing software code. True artificial Intelligence will not be achieved this way for perhaps a decade or two. We believe we've discovered a way to shorten the timeframe for such an event," Dr. Arnstadt explained.

Rick and I exchanged looks. Fortunately we both were in complete control of our emotions, so it was only a glance. My heart was racing a million miles an hour. I wanted to scream, but I sat there and smiled and took several slow deep breaths. Rick must have been doing the same thing.

"We have performed extensive work in the area of neuroscience and brain chemistry however we lack the genomics knowledge to make the final connections. We believe between your research department and your genomics department, your firm can provide the missing pieces of the puzzle," Dr. Arnstadt concluded.

"So Mr. Flannigan, are you interested in helping us?" Mr. Hess asked.

"Well of course we are! I just have some questions. We want to make sure we can actually help you and your colleagues in this project." Rick said.

"First, I have to ask: what are your intentions for such a technology, Mr. Hess?" Rick asked.

"Are you asking for my business plan, Mr. Flannigan?" Mr. Hess replied very curtly, glaring at him.

"No sir. I didn't mean it that way. I meant have you developed ideas for a practical application or more than one application for that matter? I'm only asking because it will help me and my team to better understand what we're trying to do. We need to know how we are helping and for what," Rick asked.

"We have two basic goals for this project Mr. Flannigan. The first goal is to pioneer the bioelectrical connections between our quantum computer and a human brain. If we are successful with this aspect of our project, it will open new avenues of product development that will benefit all people. Can you imagine an electric heart? How about a biomechanical pancreas or liver or kidney? Imagine a skeletal structure fused with computer circuitry! The combinations are endless once you overcome the immune system," Mr. Hess explained.

Our second goal is more ambitious. We expect that our software algorithms will serve to create a mind map of a human brain. Our software will have the capability to observe human brain actions and to replicate the development of the neural network dynamics, but in the software! It will learn to replicate a human brain using software algorithms alongside its own programs. The implication of that possibility is unimaginable!" he said and then fell silent.

"Here's the thing: A human brain contains a few hundred million axon/dendrite connections. Our program will make it possible for us to create in essence, a synthetic brain or computer brain with billions and billions of axon/dendrite connections! The thinking ability is staggering!" Dr. Arnstadt shared.

"Exactly where do you see us fitting into your program?" Rick asked.

"Our team has developed what you might call a synthetic neural network, designed to connect with the dendrites found in a human brain. Of course we've already tested the components on lab animals, you know, mice, rats, and chimps. It works to a point and then…it doesn't work anymore!" Mr. Hess explained.

"We need your firm to help integrate our hardware with the brain of a biological host. Our team has failed to discover why the biology is not working. There's a problem there with the brain rejecting the synthetic neural axons. We believe you and your team can solve that problem for us," Mr. Hess added.

"Where are you going to get a brain?" Rick asked.

"Please leave that to us Mr. Flannigan. We've made preparations for that portion of the project," Mr. Hess added.

"Do you have a timeframe for your project Mr. Hess?" Rick asked.

"Yes. We have been developing this project for years, at least developing the foundation of knowledge and test data. Last year we moved the entire study into a project status. About eight weeks ago, we ran into problems with our testing, and decided we needed outside help. We've interviewed with several other reputable biotech firms, but their expertise did not match well with our project, so we find ourselves here today with you," Mr. Hess replied.

"When do you envision that our group would get involved with the project? When would we need to get started?" Rick asked again.

"Right away Mr. Flannigan! Right away. The sooner the better. We have no time to waste," Mr. Hess replied.

"Well, we'd need to review the current data you've been using for your testing. We'll get started once we had time to review your lab notes. We would need at least four weeks for our preliminary study and then we can meet again to develop an actual timeline for production," Rick said.

"That will suit our needs Mr. Flannigan. You'll have your data in two days and we'll be in touch," Mr. Hess said.

With that all three men stood up. We shook hands and they left. Rick and I returned to his office and shut the door.

"What do you think Doug?" Rick asked with a big smile on his face.

"Are you crazy? Sorry, are you crazy boss?" I said turning red with fear.

"Doug, this sounds interesting," Rick replied. He was cool as a cucumber. I admired his ability to stay calm. I wish I was more like him.

"I'm not sure we can help these guys and besides, Mr. Hess seems like he would be a difficult client. He looks like someone who doesn't accept failure very graciously," I added, realizing the depth of fear that man invoked in me.

"Doug, we were very up front with him regarding our deliverables. He seemed to understand our hesitation and our concerns that we may not be successful. With the work we are doing for Walter Harrison and this contract, we stand to make a great deal of money Doug! Consider the new potential patents and bragging rights. These two projects could make our company big-time! Here's the best part Doug…both companies are asking for almost identical research. We haven't signed any exclusive agreement with either company! There's no downside to this new deal!" Rick said with a huge smile on his face.

"I'll have to think about this a little more about this second deal. I just want to go on record with you Rick that my gut has a bad feeling about Mr. Hess and company." I replied.

"I just don't see how we can do both projects! We'll all end up sleeping here in the lab. We'll be lucky if we get any sleep at all!" I said desperately.

"It'll work itself out Doug. You'll see," Rick said with the confidence of a great CEO.

I left Rick's office with a sense of dread. Could this guy be the person Gabe was telling me about? Could Mr. Hess actually be Levant? I was so sure it was Walter! This guy makes Walter look like the pope! He sure seemed to fit the profile that Gabe described. I wonder what he was up to with his project. Maybe this was the next move Gabe was telling me about. On the other hand, I've always trusted Rick's judgment. I wish I could talk to Rick about my involvement with the aliens. He'd know what was going on. He'd know what to do.

Rick's always made prudent decisions and is a great judge of character. He doesn't seem too worried about these guys. Maybe I'm being overcautious. Maybe my time with the aliens has affected my own judgment somehow. Maybe I am actually crazy! I just don't know anymore.

Two days later Rick received the files in an email. We spent three full days sequestered in his office pouring over the details. What we saw was shocking to both of us. There were so many intricate details and schematics that graphically mapped out the connections. There was a separate file for the synthetic axons and their ideas and guesses about how they thought the interface would work. Some of their ideas were exactly correct and others seemed to wander along without a logical conclusion. They simply had not figured some of the key components of the equations they were using. That's where we come in. It would be our task to resolve the missing sections of their equations.

197

As we worked through each section, both Rick and I began to develop our own ideas and questions about this project. After two days, Rick couldn't take the suspense anymore and said:

"Doug, are you getting a sense for how powerful this technology will be if it's successful?"

"I've been thinking the same thing. If we are successful with this project, our companies will have the power and skills to migrate human beings into artificial environments! We can create true cyborgs! Is the world ready for such a change?" I asked staggered by the implications of our discussion.

"It, it would mean an actual end to human death!" Rick said, realizing the profound impact this project would have on humanity.

"My God Doug! This is bigger than huge! This is revolutionary! This will change everything. The money almost doesn't matter," Rick said his mind racing a million miles an hour.

"It's an exciting thought and also a very sobering thought Rick. For the first time in history humankind will take their destiny into their own hands. Our species will have an opportunity to become immortal!" I said giddy from the sobering realities we were discussing. Rick and I could clearly see the scientific pathway we would travel and saw the goal, the end results. We would go down in history as the discoverers of the fountain of youth!

My team was sworn to secrecy on both projects. We rolled up our sleeves and got to work. There were two separate sets of lab notes, one for Walter and his group and the other set for Mr. Hess and his group. The research they were asking for was almost identical. Both projects were unsettling to me in light of my involvement with the aliens. My mind kept mulling over the astronomical coincidence that two major clients would walk through our doors within a few months of each other and both clients would request almost identical services from us. Both projects would be almost impossible to complete. It was a million to one shot that we could complete either project.

Rick and I both knew this going in, but we also knew we'd be paid handsomely even if we failed. And if we did fail, at least we would come out the other end with a ton of patentable data. There was really very little downside for the company from a business perspective. From my perspective, I could feel the strands of my life furiously weaving together forming a dark sinister pattern. My heart harbored quiet fears that I would not enjoy the final outcome. There was nothing to do but continue in my work and hope that Gabe and company would be looking out for me and my family.

There was one more thing, another aspect to this whole new piece of business that was unsettling. Mr. Hess had no ethical concerns about using a human brain for his new invention! It was strictly business with him and business at any cost. I thought of Jim and his association with the aliens and his nickname...Dr. Frankenstein. After meeting Mr. Hess I felt like I had actually met the real Dr. Frankenstein. So many questions and doubts flooded into my head and my heart driving to and from work. Who was Levant? What if our program actually succeeds? What if they both succeed? What if Walter and Mr. Hess ever met? What will they say when they find out we've been helping them both?

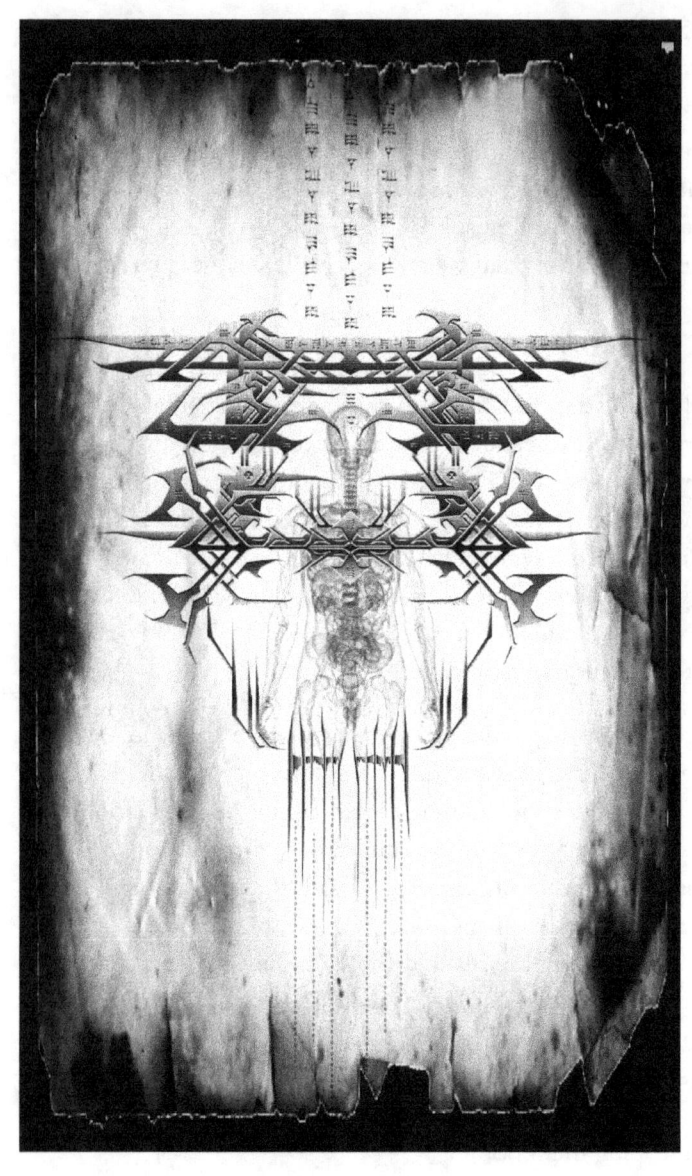

"INVOLUNTARY CYBERNETIC RE-ANIMATION"

Chapter 15

The following week the entire team met for a recap of our current progress on the Galaxy project and to make plans for the final implementation. We met at the Galaxy office in Los Angeles. Rick and I traveled down from Fresno and made sure we were at least two hours early to the meeting. When we arrived Bob and Jim were already there.

"Morning gentlemen," Rick said as we walked through the doors of the executive conference room.

"Good morning Rick. Good morning Doug," Bob said.

"Gentlemen! Glad you are here," Jim added. "Walter will join us shortly," Jim said. Walter came in a few minutes later and we started the meeting.

"Good morning Walter," Rick said as Walter slid into his chair at the end of the conference table.

"Good morning Rick. Good morning Doug. I'm sorry I'm late. Please proceed," Walter said with a warm smile.

"As I was explaining, Doug's team has made remarkable progress developing the biological components of the project. In my opinion, they've just performed a miracle of science! The team started with a series of living stem cells and then engineered them into becoming brain cells! The results have been spectacular and really beyond what any of us dreamed could be possible. Our team has, in fact, grown an organic human brain!" Rick said beaming with joy.

"The brain is alive. It's healthy! We've conducted electrical testing to insure its working and it is...working. The strange thing is this- the brain has never been part of a human body. It's never had an experience outside of our lab tests. It's a blank slate Walter! We don't know what it will do once it's connected to NOAH," Rick finished and sat down. Nobody spoke. The room was silent and then Walter spoke up.

"Outstanding job Rick, I knew you guys would do this for us," he said smiling.

"As we have already discussed, this project will take us all into uncharted waters. Science and medicine have only imagined what we are attempting to do here with our project. Let's hope this process will give us the prize we're after. I have complete confidence that NOAH and his programs will help support this new life form. I believe he will be our hope in working through this next phase and also with the neural plasticity variable," Walter said.

"We've completed the testing on the chip implant. It connects perfectly to NOAH using the RF Wi-Fi. We've taken the liberty to add some redundancies. There are actually six different RF bands that provide connections. They serve double duty in that data transfers can be spread over all six bands and if a band should disconnect, NOAH and Eve will still be connected with the other five bands," Walter explained.

"Our testing results with the biological dendrites and synthetic axons have stabilized and we are close to a ninety nine percent positive connection rate, We believe we are very close to the procedure to connect Eve to NOAH. We would expect a percentage of the connections to fail initially, but much like a human brain, we need to allow time to study the dynamics of

202

the neural plasticity. Our expectation is that NOAH and Eve will work these parts out together. They'll need to learn to do that anyway. There should be no rejection or infection anticipated." Rick added.

"Where are you planning on conducting the testing?" Rick asked Walter.

"We have a small, yet well-equipped medical facility tucked away in one of our operational sites." Walter replied. "We knew this day would come and we've made preparations to assemble a full medical staff. We've also constructed a surgery room and hospital recovery area. I can assure you Doug; we've taken every precaution for this part of the program," Walter shared, looking right at me when he spoke.

"Where is this facility located?" Rick asked.

"It's close Rick. We wanted to make sure that you and your team would be close when we approached this final phase. None of our overseas facilities would have served as well," Walter added.

"Well, can we see it? Have you set up a lab area for me and my staff?" Rick asked.

"Yes of course!" Walter responded. "In fact, if there's time, well take you and Doug there today. We need your recommendations for final preparations anyway," Walter said.

After lunch, Walter took us to the facility as promised. It was out in the desert about thirty miles west of Mojave. The whole place was unassuming. It looked more like a broken down ranch or abandoned mining operation than a medical facility. The front gate on the side of the freeway was the only road leading to the compound. It was obvious from the rust it had been part of the original equipment. We traveled almost a mile toward an outcropping of small hills. The compound was secured with a new six foot security fence completer with razor wire running across the top.

The buildings were all built near the turn of the century or maybe a little later. They were old and unassuming. Maybe this had been a mining operation at one time. The place was creepy and reminded me of Emma's Chuck Wagon. We stopped in front of the largest building and went inside. As we approached the entrance, Rick and I were surprised to see several armed guards at the front door. Looking past the guards the interior was completely modern. It could have been a small hospital anywhere. As we toured the facility, we were impressed with the scope of the preparations. The place was a fully functioning hospital! It would be capable of handling any contingency we would face. It was also a little creepy that this hospital was out here in the middle of nowhere!

The drive back to the office was filled with questions and answers regarding the facility. I felt uneasy that Rick and I hadn't been told about this place until so late in the game. Driving back to Fresno from Los Angeles, Rick and I didn't talk much. I suspect he was feeling the weight of the moral aspects of this last part of the program. I know I was. Sometimes in science, the lines get blurred. We always want to succeed, to create something beneficial for humankind, and sometimes we take our eye off the doing the right thing.

I was weighing the moral ramifications of what we were involved in and quite sure that Rick was doing the same thing. There was some comfort knowing we weren't sacrificing a living person, but still, we had created an almost whole organic brain! We termed it artificial, but for all practical purposes, it was a real human brain. What's going to happen when "Eve" becomes self-aware? That was the moral question rattling around our heads and hearts as we drove home.

Both of us had been in this territory before. It wasn't too many years ago when we endured the whole embryonic stem cell fiasco. Our firm was ready to go with major research using embryonic stem cells, but the government shut down our supply and that program ended. Rick and I both felt the morality of that issue was weighted in the wrong direction. We resented the government for not allowing us to continue the research. But it wasn't to be, so we pulled the plug and moved the company in a different direction. Now we were back into the gray area once again with this project. I didn't like the fact that we would be operating out of a clandestine hospital out in the middle of nowhere. It didn't feel right. Why should it?

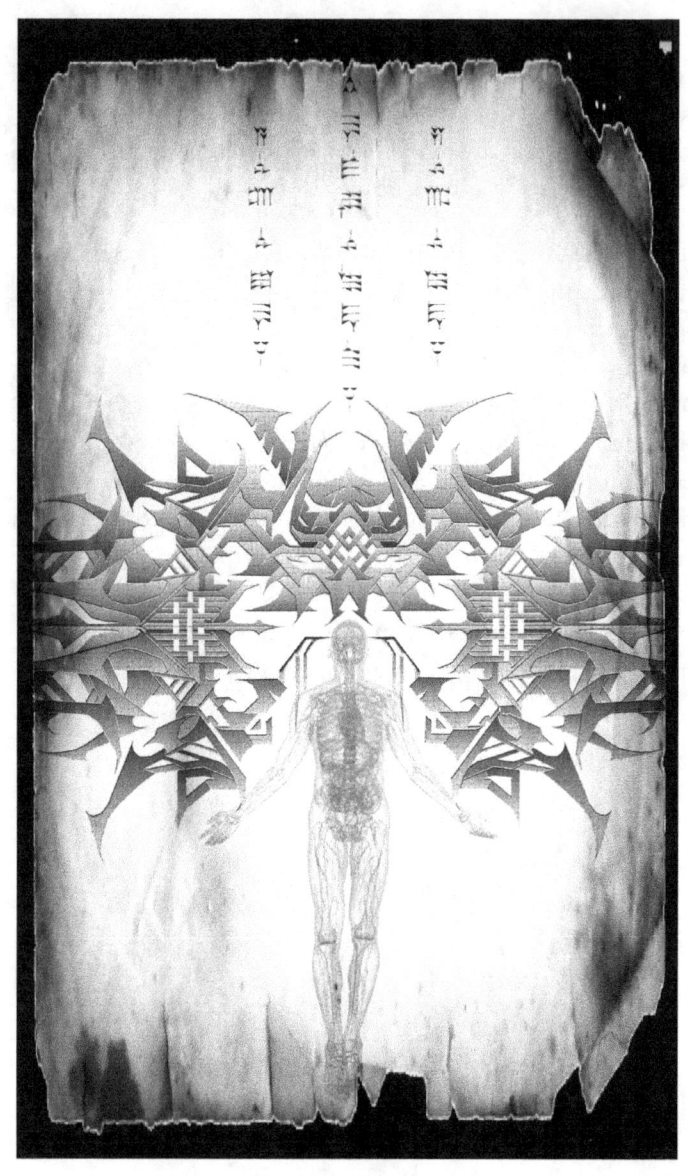

"PROJECT OMEGA | BIOMETRIC TRANSFERRENCE"

Chapter 16

Two weeks later Mr. Hess and his associates showed up at our office. They wanted to see our progress. Rick and I were both shocked to see them. They had not set an appointment or called, but simply walked through the front door. Rick immediately stopped what he was doing and invited them into his office, motioning for me to come in as well. Once inside we all sat down and Mr. Hess started the conversation:

"Mr. Flannigan, we need to review the data we sent you and answer any questions you may have developed," Mr. Hess said very pointedly.

"Well we do have a list of questions," Rick replied as we all sat down at the conference table.

"My associates and I have some ethical concerns with respect to using a human subject for this project. Can you elaborate on the circumstances of finding someone interested in such a venture?" Rick asked.

"Certainly Mr. Flannigan, we are not animals. We have morals and ethical values as well. Our volunteer must remain anonymous outside this room. I will say that he is a very brilliant man and has enjoyed a very successful career in science. He is also suffering from a rare form of cancer that will end his life soon. Our hope and his hope as well, is that if we succeed in our project, that he will be given the time to work on finding a cure for his disease. To be exact, he has less than a year to live. Considering his current level of knowledge and the fact that his brain will have access to a quantum computer, a year is a very long time to search out a potential cure." Mr. Hess explained.

Rick and I looked at each other and then back at Mr. Hess. His explanation was somewhat rational and calming and at the same time…it was alarming! There was a very humanist element in holding out tangible hope to a person facing certain death. On the other hand, part of me felt like we would be taking advantage of a desperate person for our own gain. How is it that we always find ourselves in the burning crucible of justice struggling to weigh right from wrong? Why was it always so difficult to make these decisions?

"Well Mr. Hess. That explains a lot and I feel much relieved hearing that our project might actually save someone's life rather than take it," Rick replied.

"Our subject, who has graciously accepted our offer, will create an experiment within an experiment. If he is successful, he will save his own life, but he will also save the lives of countless others as well. My company will benefit from his research and allow us to grow our new business division as well as our pharmaceutical division. The truth is Mr. Flannigan this project may offer humanity a solution to most of their problems. It's not much unlike the story of Dr. Frankenstein and his monster. The man was dead and was brought back to life! I'm prone to believe we are creating a new future for the human race with our project," Mr. Hess added.

I felt the temperature in the room rise very quickly. His words shot through me like a lightning bolt burning me up from the inside out. My first instinct was to run for the door, but I didn't. My legs were twitching and I took a couple of deep breaths and tried to calm myself. I gulped my whole glass of water in a single gulp! As I placed my glass on the table I noticed Mr. Hess studying me and smiling a very faint smile. How did he know that? How did he know those words would unsettle me? Why does this guy seem to be inside my head knowing my every thought? As I collected myself I looked back at him and smiled. I knew he was Levant!

"One more small detail for you and your team, lest you think of me as a monster: the subject is my older brother! I love him dearly and cannot afford to lose his brilliant mind. What other questions do you have for us today Mr. Flannigan?" Mr. Hess asked calmly, glancing at Rick and then back at me. My mind went into shock hearing Mr. Hess's story. His brother! I looked nervously at Rick. He was calm as a cucumber.

"We have made progress from the data you sent us. We believe we can solve your problems. In fact, we've already made breakthroughs on several of them. Where, uh, where are you planning on conducting this, I mean, performing the final connections? Where will the surgery take place?" Rick asked with a nervous tone in his voice.

"We have a small operation near the Austrian- Hungarian border. The facility suits us well as it is somewhat remote, yet easy to get to. It's also close to home for me and my associates. My legal staff has taken care of any legal issues and the local authorities have been well managed, so there will be no problems I can assure you," Mr. Hess explained.

"Okay. I understand. Do you have a schedule for the operation? We will still need a little time to put the final pieces in place. We will then need to review all the final results and coordinate the final solution for the surgery," Rick said.

"We expect to schedule the operation not more than six weeks from now. We have some leeway, but prefer to begin the final phase in six weeks," Mr. Hess stated.

"I think that will work for us Mr. Hess," Rick replied.

"Any more questions Mr. Flannigan?" Mr. Hess asked.

"No. No I think you've answered the big ones for us," Rick replied.

"Very well then; we will plan to meet back here in thirty days, review the final solution, and prepare for the surgery in Hungary," Mr. Hess said. We all stood up and Rick shook Mr. Hess's hand. I nodded and smiled to all of them as they made their way to the front door. I watched them leaving our office and the sight of them leaving lifted a great weight from me.

Just then, Walter and Jim walked through the front door! Rick and I both saw them at the same time. We held our breath. It was unnerving watching the two groups of men pass each other in the narrow space near the front door. The scene was surreal and unfolded in slow motion as Walter and Mr. Hess passed each other. They both looked each other over thoroughly, exchanging curt smiles, not knowing who the other man was or the reason for their presence in our office.

Rick and I paused momentarily until we saw Hess and company swing out the front door.

"Walter! Jim! What a pleasant surprise. We weren't expecting to see you guys today," Rick said with a broad smile and outstretched hand.

"Gentlemen! How are you doing today? Jim and I were in the neighborhood and thought we'd stop by," Walter said, shaking my hand.

"Hi Walter, hi Jim," I said as I shook hands with them both.

"Please come into my office," Rick said.

The four of us went into Rick's office and sat at the conference table.

"We're not interrupting anything are we?" Walter asked.

"No! Not at all Walter," Rick replied.

"New clients?" Walter asked throwing his head toward the front door and giving us a sideways glance.

"Possibly, we've had a couple of preliminary meetings with them. We'll see what happens. You know this business…you never know what's going to happen next," Rick said laughing off his nervousness and calming down.

"So what can we do for you two gents today?" Rick asked.

"We were in the area and thought we'd stop by and see if we can discuss a date for the final step in the project. Our team is ready and standing by," Walter shared.

"Well, Doug and I have been going over our testing results and we believe we will be ready to go in two weeks. Does that timeframe work for you Walter?" Rick asked.

"Yes. That works perfectly! Let's schedule the operation fourteen days from now and plan to remain onsite for three to four days to monitor the operation and provide any follow up that's needed," Walter said.

"Then we're set. We've got a date Walter!" Rick smiled and they both shook hands. Jim and I shook hands and I shook Walter's hand as they said their goodbyes and walked out.

Two minutes later, Rick and I just looked at each other in disbelief.

"Can you believe what just happened?" he asked.

"Doug, that was a close call to a potentially embarrassing situation," Rick added.

"Rick, what happens if we're successful with both projects?" I asked him with some concern.

"What do you mean Doug?" Rick asked.

"I mean if we are successful with both operations, both companies will go out into the world and dominate their respective fields using nearly identical technologies. My question is this: what will happen to us when they both find out we were partners with both of them pursing almost identical goals? What happens then?" I asked almost desperate as the meaning of my own words began to settle in.

"Nothing Doug! We don't have a problem. We sell a product. People come to us when they need our expertise in genomics, medicines, or human physiology. We did not sign any non-compete agreement with either company. We also did not sign a mutually exclusive agreement with either company. We only signed non-disclosure agreements with them. The proprietary data we developed for them belongs to us. Besides, if there's any

212

problem with either of them, I suspect they'll go after each other," Rick explained and smiled.

"Come on buddy! We got this one," Rick said trying to lighten my mood. It didn't work.

I went home that night more confused than I can remember. Both projects were coming along. Both projects had workable deadline dates. Rick was okay with all the arrangements, but I could feel the future coming and it wasn't good. It was almost a premonition of something very bad. I didn't trust Mr. Hess and his associates. My gut was telling me he was Levant. Where was Gabe? What was he doing? Is Gabe able to monitor me and my family somehow? Is he aware that Levant has surfaced? I went to bed worried and didn't sleep very well.

The next two days were busy days making final preparations for Walter's project. I drifted from report to report reviewing everything, but my heart wasn't in it. I couldn't shake the nervousness. On the third day Rick burst into my office and said:

"Doug! We need to talk right now! Let's go to my office," Rick said. He was terrified which almost sent me over the edge. I can't take much more of this drama!

"Mr. Hess and his associates are dead! Their jet crashed somewhere over the Atlantic!" Rick said with a wild look on his face.

"I slumped into a chair in a state of shock. Rick's words were echoing off the walls inside my brain. They were dead? They were dead! Hess was dead. Gabe! I looked at Rick as if he could read my mind.

"What happened? What are the authorities saying? How did you find this out? What does this mean Rick?" I blurted out. My head was all fogged up with this news. It was over! Levant was gone! I could feel the tension and dread draining out of me. Gabe came through for me...for my family! Suddenly I wanted to see Gabe. I wanted to hug him and thank him for saving me.

"Doug! Doug! Are you listening to me?" Rick yelled and brought me back into focus.

"Yeah, yeah I'm listening. I just don't understand. What happened? Do they know the cause of the crash?" I asked refocusing on Rick.

"I don't know any details. Mr. Hess's office in Europe called me and gave me the news. They've asked us to return all the data we were given. They've also invoked a section in the contract that said if anything happened to Mr. Hess, his office had the power to terminate the contract," Rick said.

"I guess that piece of business is gone," he added.

"What will we do Rick?" I asked.

"We'll give them their data back and continue with Walter's project. I didn't really care for Mr. Hess, but business is business. I'm sorry they died. It would have been a great opportunity for us," Rick said.

I stared at Rick and marveled at his even tempered approach to this roller coaster ride we were on. Something was tugging at my mind: Were they really dead? Was this some kind of trick Levant was playing on us all to throw us off? Why? What purpose could he have for staging something like this? Why would he want

214

everyone to think he's dead? Maybe he was dead. Where is Gabe? I really need to speak with Gabe.

"THE SHATTERING OF HUMAN BONDS"

Chapter 17

At the end of the week I got a surprise phone call from Bob. "Doug! It's me Bob. Hey I need to see you. We need to talk. I have to tell you what's going on. It's not good." Bob explained.

"What do you mean 'not good?'" I asked.

"I need to talk to you in person. I got fired today, but there's a lot going on at Galaxy that you don't know about. I need to talk to you in person!" Bob said with emphasis.

"I can't get away tomorrow or Friday, but maybe we can meet over the weekend. When and where?" I asked. "Let's meet at Denny's in Riverton," Bob suggested.

"Really Bob!" I replied. "What's wrong with Denny's?" Bob asked.

"Nothing Bob. Nothing. What time?" I asked. Let's meet at 11 A.M. Does that work for you?" Bob asked.

"Yeah. I'll make it work," I replied.

Mary was looking at me with a puzzling look when I hung up the phone.

"What's going on?" she asked.

"That was Bob. He wants to meet with me on Saturday, in Riverton," I added.

"Is everything okay," she asked.

"Yeah! It's okay. It's just this project we're working on. He needs to review some of the data with me. We have to be ready by Monday," I said, hoping to calm her down. I didn't want Mary worried or upset by any of this. Somehow I'd deal with it. I couldn't tell her about Bob being fired. Not yet.

When I pulled into Denny's parking lot, Bob was waiting in his car. When he saw me drive up, he got out and met me as I was locking my car.

"What's up Bob," I asked.

"Let's go inside. I have a ton of stuff to tell you," he said with a look of loss on his face. His look startled me and I began to prepare myself for what Bob was going to tell me. We went inside and grabbed a table.

"Doug, you and Rick don't have the whole story on Walter's project! Walter and Jim have a whole different program they're preparing to roll out. I only discovered their plan the day after our last meeting. I'm not sure what their goal is, but I didn't like the parts I was hearing about," Bob said with a look of desperation on his face.

"Like what? What are they planning to do with this project? What did you discover? Wait, did they tell you this?" I asked.

"No! Neither of them said anything to me!" Bob explained.

"So tell me, how did you discover this information?" I asked becoming a little nervous about our conversation.

"I was in Jim's office. We were discussing different aspects of the project when Jim asked me to get some documents he'd put on my desk. So I went back to my office, got the documents,

218

and when I returned, Jim was gone. I set the docs on his desk and as I was leaving, I saw a thumb-drive on the floor. I picked it up, but I didn't put it back on his desk. Something inside me said to keep it! So I did. When I got back to my office, I immediately downloaded the thumb-drive into my notebook and took it back to Jim's office. I put it back on the floor where I found it." Bob said.

"When I got home from work, I opened the file and what I learned shocked me!" Bob said with a look of panic in his voice.

"What was it? What was in the file?" I asked urging Bob to speed up his story.

"Well, you know the goal was to integrate the chip implant with the organic brain you were engineering? The goal was to create a hybrid biological unit that could interface with NOAH and at the same time, could effectively oversee the whole operation. The chip implant would have guaranteed that Eve and NOAH would grow and evolve together. NOAH would have access to Eve's brain and would have used the mind map algorithms to learn to replicate the axon-dendrite connections. But that's not the purpose for the program," Doug said

"The real purpose of the program was to establish a phase one platform for Walter's plan to make subtle changes to the whole human race! Doug, this guy thinks he's God or something! He's crazy! His plan is, once he can launch NOAH and Eve, he can begin gathering crucial and personal information on everyone on the planet, at least the ones that use a cellphone or the Internet. The second phase of his plan seemed a little strange to me. The file said that Eve would soon gain the ability to begin downloading information into the collective unconsciousness of all humanity. I had never heard of such a thing! The file stated

219

that once all the trials were completed, that NOAH and Eve would begin to introduce information via Eve's human consciousness to the collective unconscious! I'm not completely sure what al that means, but it sounds to me like Walter and Jim are planning to take over the world!" Bob said with his eyes bulging and gasping for air.

"What did you just say?" I asked. I was stunned at what Bob had just told me.

"Did you say that Walter intends to use Eve, NOAH, and the project to download information into the collective unconscious?" I asked.

"Yes. That's exactly what they are planning," Bob replied.

"There's something else too. Walter was never planning to use your organic brain for his project! He's planning on using a human host!"

It all made sense now. That's why Jim was there. Jim was an expert on this stuff and Walter, Walter was the devil himself! Walter was Levant! I knew that for sure now.

"There's more Doug," Bob said.

"The project is way ahead of where you and Rick think it is. They've actually installed the chip implant in a test subject months ago. I'm not sure what went wrong with that experiment. They never told me about it, but I found out about it when I was reviewing some notes on the thumb drive." Bob shared. "It was interesting that the unit worked perfectly as designed in that the remote unit was able to communicate flawlessly with NOAH. There was something else though that Walter was looking for. He was expecting the new unit to help integrate suggestions into the collective unconscious. Don't ask me to explain how he could measure such a thing, but he seemed to know what he was looking for, at least according to the notes I saw." Bob said.

"So you think that Walter is looking for a different host, one that has some kind of ability to connect with the collective unconsciousness in a way that will allow Walter to download information into the collective unconsciousness?" I asked. I already knew the answer to the question. I was thinking out loud and trying to figure out how Ruth and I figured into Walter's plan. My gut was telling me he was planning to come for us, but how? That's what I didn't know.

"Yes! That's exactly what he intends to do. Imagine the power he would have over, well, everyone! He could eventually decide what people would think and how they would feel about things! That guy is a madman! We've got to stop him Doug! Somehow, we've got to figure out a way to end this project," Bob said with a desperate tone in his voice.

"Somehow I've got to bring Rick in on this. He has to know what's going on and maybe together, the three of us can stop the project," I said. "Tell me, Bob, how does Jim figure into this project? What do you know about him?" I asked.

"Jim has been a friend of Walter's for about twenty years. They go way back. He's worked for other companies, but he came to work for Galaxy a few years back. He's got doctorate in neuroscience and a second doctorate in astrophysics! He's basically a walking genius!" Bob shared. "Anyway, they've been inseparable for a year or two. Jim travels with him all over the world," Bob said. They've both been very hands-on on this project," he added

"Okay Bob. I need to get back home and meet with Rick. I think we can put some pressure on Walter and at least slow down the project until we can figure out how to abort it," I said. I was thinking this would give me some time to contact Gabe and hopefully Gabe had a plan and would help us stop Walter's plan. At the moment, I didn't know what other moves we could make. We agreed to talk at the end of the day tomorrow. I would fill him in on my meeting with Rick and we would begin to make a plan to stop Walter and Jim.

When I got home it was late. The kids were in bed already, but Mary was still up. I had to tell her everything, well, almost everything. I told her everything I knew about Walter's plan, including that I was planning to meet with Rick and that together with Bob we were going to somehow stop Walter, A.K.A. Levant, one of the most powerful beings in the universe and who couldn't actually be killed! I didn't tell Mary that last part. I was secretly hoping that Gabe and Micah had some kind of a death ray gun or kryptonite bullet or something like that to stop Levant and just didn't bother to tell me because it was some kind of higher species galactic secret weapon that I didn't need to know about. I was hoping all of this as I told Mary my plans, leaving out the death ray stuff.

Mary listened patiently to everything I told her. She asked some questions and finally said:

" Doug, I'm not sure what God has planned for this whole thing, but somehow it will work out," She said with a quiet confidence. I was stunned! Is this my wife talking? I expected her to be upset and panicked, but she was wasn't.

"Mary, I'm not too sure what God has to do with this situation, so I'm not completely sure He's going to help us here!" I said

222

trying to humor her. She obviously did not fully understand what I was dealing with here. It didn't have anything to do with God or her church or anything religious at all. This was nothing more than a colossal power grab by a ruthless alien who was trying to take over the world. Levant was trying to steal human consciousness for whatever purpose he had in mind. It was just that simple to me. I was quietly pleased that my wife was not undone or making a scene. I was also quietly amazed at the strength of her faith in God! Her support was awesome!

What I didn't tell Mary is that I would stay up late tonight and tune into channel 777 on the television and hope that somebody was listening. Maybe if I could connect with Gabe and company, they could help me with my plan to stop Walter. I waited until Mary went to sleep and turned the television to channel 777. The next thing I knew it was morning and no contact from Gabe. Why didn't he contact me? Where is he? Why is he ignoring me when I need him the most? I took a shower and got ready for work. I'd speak with Rick today and lay out the whole scenario for him and get his thoughts on our next move.

When I had told him the whole story Rick was completely undone. His initial reaction was to get our lawyers involved, which was a move we simply couldn't make.

"Rick, this is something we have to take care of ourselves. It has to be done quietly, privately by us. There's no legal action for us to pursue here," I pleaded.

"Then exactly what do you suggest we do Doug?" Rick yelled, obviously frustrated at the predicament we were in.

"I think we need to meet face to face with Walter and tell him what we know and voice our objections and then demand that we sever our relationship with him and his company. That way they cannot use any of our technology, nor do we have to be party to any of the end goals they seem to be planning," I said.

Rick made the call and set up the meeting with Walter. We'd meet in our office in two days and put an end to the whole project; at least an end to our participation in it and that was good enough for me. Two days later, Walter and Jim showed up in Rick's office. We all met in the conference room and Rick explained to Walter that we wanted out of the contract and what we were prepared to do if he refused our request. This was where I was expecting the fight to happen. I thought Walter would explode and demand that we remain in the project and threaten to sue the hell out of us, but he didn't. He smiled!

Walter smiled a quiet smile and told Rick that he had enjoyed doing business with us. He said he was disappointed in Rick's decision, but he understood. He said he understood our concerns about the direction of the project and would honor our request to break the contract. When he was finished talking, he stood up, smiled warmly at Rick, shook his hand, and walked out of the room. Jim followed him and hadn't said a word during the whole meeting.

Rick looked at me and sighed a big sigh of relief.

"Wow! I'm glad that went well. I'm glad that this is over," he said, slouching into his chair. I just looked at him wondering what had just happened and what it meant. Rick thought this was some kind of a business deal, but I knew now that it was much more than that. Walter had something up his sleeve. There was something else going on. I just didn't know what his next move was going to be. I went back to my office and shut the door.

My cell phone rang and it was Mary.

"Ruth is missing!" she screamed into the phone.

"What? What do you mean missing?" I asked feeling my heart pounding.

"I mean her pre-school called and said she was missing! They said she was there for most of the morning and then they couldn't find her. She vanished!" Mary said. "Doug, you've got to come right now. We have to find her!" Mary screamed into the phone.

"I'm on my way right now!" I yelled back.

I felt the blood drain out of my body as I grabbed my keys and headed for the door. Where is Ruth? Where could she be? I tried to calm myself down as I drove to the pre-school, but it wasn't possible. All I could do was mutter to myself, God please help her. Please! Please! Help us find her. Let her be safe with a friend. By the time I pulled into the parking lot at the pre-school I was a little calmer, at least on the outside. I had to be. Mary was waiting for me as I walked through the door.

"Oh God Doug! I can't believe this. They said that Ruth was here and then, just like that, she was gone. Nobody saw anybody or anything," she wailed to me.

"Let's take this one step at a time Mary. Let's talk to Ellen and see what she can tell us," I said as we walked into the pre-school office.

Ellen Merton was a sensible lady who ran a very tight pre-school. Mary and I both had total faith and trust in Ellen and the way she ran her school. She met both of us right away.

"Ellen, what happened? How can Ruth be missing?" I asked as calmly as I was able.

"Doug. Mary. Ruth was with us all day since Mary dropped her off this morning at a little before 9am. After lunch Ruth went to use the restroom, but she never came back. We've checked all the video cameras and checked with Mr. Harkness, our security officer, but there was nothing on the cameras and Mr. Harkness said he never saw anyone come in or leave. We don't know where she is! We don't know how she could have gotten out of here without being seen or photographed," Ellen explained.

"Of course we called the police. The moment we knew she was missing, we called them. The police won't take a missing person's report until they've been missing for twenty four hours. Our next call was to Mary," Ellen said.

Mary and I went to the police station and gave our statements and a photo of Ruth. We picked up the boys from school and drove home. Mary was set on calling all our friends and all of Ruth's friends to see if by any chance she could be with one of them. It slowly began to sink in to me that something else could have happened to Ruth. I didn't want to think about it, but it kept forcing its way into my mind. Levant could have taken Ruth! I couldn't bear to think the thought, but it just kept popping into my head. Why would he take her? He was supposed to take me! Maybe he took her so he could get me. That's it! That has to be it. I couldn't tell Mary. I needed to think of something. What to do? What would I do? What should I do? I wasn't sure. I had no idea what to do.

I had to contact Gabe. He had to get my signal. He just had to. He's the only one who can help us now. It was a very tense night at home. Mary would not go to sleep. How could she? I couldn't sleep either. I wanted to dial the television to channel 777, but Mary wouldn't leave my side. Neither of us slept a wink the entire night. My only hope was to drive to Riverton and hope I could get to Emma's and hoped I could make contact with Gabe. He could help us.

When the sun came up I felt a little relief. I took a shower and made coffee.

"Mary, I'm going out to look for Ruth. I don't know what else to do. I need you to stay by the phone in the hopes that someone calls with news of Ruth," I said as calmly as I could. Mary understood the whole thing and agreed to do as I asked. I told her I'd be home by dark and hopefully our nightmare would end on a happy note. At times like these it's so hard to be hopeful. I had to have hope. Hope is all we have to cling to without falling into the oblivion of inconsolable grief and darkness.

I drove out of town knowing exactly where I was going. With a little luck I could get to Emma's and Gabe and he would help us. There was a lot to think about during my drive to Riverton. I was calmer today, although the sickness in my gut wasn't any better. I felt calmer and more level-headed and focused on crunching the data and getting my little girl back safe and sound.

What I've figured out is that Levant had to be behind this. I don't think anyone in the world would have singled out Ruth for abduction. The security at the school was too good and even they said she simply vanished. I'm assuming that Levant must have some powers I'm not aware of, and making a little girl disappear is one of them. But at least he could have done this. But why? All I could come up with is that he knew he could get me if he took my little girl.

I pulled into the Denny's parking lot in Riverton and went inside. I went immediately into the restroom, but when I came out, it was still Denny's. I took a table and ordered a coffee and a light breakfast. I waited for the coffee to come and returned to the restroom, but when I went in and came out, it was still Denny's. I wasn't prepared for this. I just knew that Gabe would be picking me up on this one. I ate my breakfast and drank two more cups of coffee. I called Bob and told him what was going on. He was shocked and concerned.

"Don't do anything Bob. Let me work on this from my end for now," I said.

"Well Doug, if you think that Walter has Ruth, we need to go get her. We both know she's probably at their secret lab in the desert," Bob said.

"Bob, just let me play my angle. I'll call you back in an hour when I know more," I said and hung up.

I made one more trip to the restroom, but it was uneventful. There was no Emma's and no Gabe. I paid my bill and got in my car and drove home.

Neither Mary nor I slept a wink all night. We were both emotionally drained. The next morning I went to work, not knowing what else to do. Maybe Walter would call. Maybe he'd make some kind of deal with me. Maybe he figured he could pressure us to complete our end of the bargain. A million different scenarios raced through my mind on the way to the office. Ten minutes after I arrived I got a phone call from Jim.

"Doug. This is Jim. Are you okay?"

"Hell no I'm not okay Jim. My daughter is missing and I'm pretty sure I know where she is!" I yelled into the phone.

"You are correct Doug. That's why I'm calling. Walter's gone crazy! He fired Bob and is threatening to fire me. I never signed up for kidnapping. I need to meet with you and Bob. Doug, you have to believe me! I was never part of this deal. I have an idea how we can get inside the compound and get Ruth back. I have access," he said panting into the phone.

"Okay, okay. I'm with you Jim. Just tell me what to do. Where and when do we meet?" I asked.

"Doug, listen to me very carefully. Call Bob and ask him to meet you in Riverton. You know the place. I can be there in four hours if I leave now. Call Bob and then meet me in Riverton in four hours. Don't say a word to anyone. I'll fill you and Bob in on my plan. If this works out like I think it will, you'll have your daughter back in ten hours," Jim explained.

"Okay Jim. I'm with you. I've got it. I'm calling Bob right now. I'll see you in four hours. Hey Jim…thanks," I said and hung up the phone.

I called Bob and told him the plan. He said he was on his way. He'd be there in four hours. I told Rick I needed to leave. He said he understood and told me to stay home for the rest of the week. I was shaking and wobbly as I walked out to the car. Maybe, just maybe, this nightmare will be over soon.

Once I hit the highway I started rolling up the miles while my mind started filling in the blanks. Of course! Why didn't I think of it? Why didn't I see this plan coming? Riverton! Emma's Café! Jim! Dr. Frankenstein! Jim was still working with Gabe. Jim was on assignment. That's why I haven't heard from Gabe. He scripted this whole situation. Of course we'd go to Emma's. Of course Jim would meet me there. We'd meet up with Gabe and Micah. We'd take the spaceship to Walter's compound and rescue Ruth! I was crying and laughing at the same time. My baby's going to be okay. Everything is going to be okay. Maybe Mary's prayers were being answered right now. Maybe there really was a God that loved us and helped us. I don't know. I don't care. I'm so grateful to finally have some hope.

When I pulled into the parking lot at Denny's I could see Jim's van parked up against the side wall of the diner. Bob's car was parked across the lot from Jim's van. I could see Jim sitting in the van looking around. He waved when he saw me. I parked next to Bob's car, and walked over to the van. Jim got out with a smile on his face and shook my hand. Then he hugged me and said:

"Hey buddy, we're going to get Ruthie back soon. You need to calm down Doug. It will be oaky. We've got help on the way," Jim said with a smile that calmed me immediately.

"Where's Bob?" I asked.

"He went to the restroom. He'll be back in a moment," Jim said.

"Look, let me show you something. Follow me." Jim said as we walked around to the back of the van.

I felt wobbly again, like the weight of the world was lifted from my shoulders and the strain my body had been under for so long and now, in an instant it was all gone! The pressure was gone. I was among friends. I was going to get help. I was going to get my baby back! I was wrong about Jim. He was a great guy and a true friend. My mind must have been clouded with emotions and as Jim opened the back door to the van he said:

"Take a look at what we've got here!"

"I stepped around the back door of the van and saw Bob lying in the back of the van! He was unconscious and tied up in duct tape. A lightning bolt of fear burned through me as I felt Jim's arm reach around and stuff something in my face and everything went dark.

"AETHYR | THE BIRTH OF CONSCIOUSNESS"

Chapter 18

When I opened my eyes the first thing I saw was Bob strapped to a table next to me. We were in some kind of operating room. The lights had been turned down very low and I could see the bright hall lights through the glass in the door. Every now and then I could see the guard look in and then walk away.

"Bob? Bob are you awake?" I whispered.

"Doug? Yeah, I'm awake. What the hell happened?" he asked.

"I think Jim drugged us and brought us here. The last thing I remember seeing was you in the back of his van. You were unconscious and tied up," I explained.

"What are we going to do Doug?" bob asked.

"I don't know Bob. Give me a minute. Let me think," I said.

I couldn't stop my mind from racing long enough to think clearly. Nobody would be coming to help us. They'd be looking for us in Riverton and the only thing they'd find there is our cars. Ruth must be here. I hope she's here. She has to be here somewhere. How do I get out of these straps? Just then the door opened. Walter and Jim walked in.

"Well, look who we have here," Walter said. "Doug, the game is over. You lost and so did you Bob," he added.

"Where is my daughter?" I growled at Walter.

"She's quite safe Doug. She is very important to us and I can assure you, we will keep her very safe." Walter said.

"Why? Why Ruth? Why not take me?" I pleaded.

"Doug, you were our number one target. You were the perfect subject for our project. You were the one we were targeting when we contacted your company. We never really needed your expertise. We already had it. Right Jim?" Walter said, smiling and looked at Jim.

"That's right boss. We've had it all along," Jim said returning the smile.

I looked at Jim and thought about how he was the one that got me into this mess. I wanted to smash his face! I wanted to kick his ass! I wanted to kill him if I could just get my hands on him. I wanted to spit in his face. The waves of hopelessness and desperation that swept over me squashed my anger and rage. Something was telling me this was not the time to reveal how I knew Jim from another time and another place. Why was he doing this? What happened in his life that caused him to turn his back on Gabe and the program? Something wasn't right here. It can't end this way!

"You see Doug, what we've discovered is that your daughter Ruth has much more connective power than you do, or than even Jim does. Oh yes, I know Jim has the same power you do, and the same power that Ruth has. What you don't know is that Ruth has ten times the empathy and connective metabolism that either of you do. Ruth's chakra signature is off the chart! She is the perfect candidate for our program and once she has been fitted with the chip implant, she will meld into the perfect blend of human, machine, and computer. She will help me broadcast the messages I need downloaded into the minds of billions of people around the world," Walter gloated.

"Doug, have you figured out yet what it is I'm after?" Walter asked, looking at me with a supremely confident smile.

"Not really Walter. Why don't you tell me your plan? What's the big payoff for you?" I asked, looking him straight in the eye.

"Doug, what all of you humans fail to realize is simply this: you are the most exquisite and pathetic creatures in the universe. You don't know yet what you have. You don't really know what life is. You think you do. You think because you go to school and learn a few things that you know something. You don't! You have all failed to recognize the value of taking a breath, of being alive, of being mortal. While being a mortal places you in a weakened and precarious situation, it also provides you with great power, power that you humans mostly don't understand. The value slides away from you until it's too late and then…you're filled with regrets. You're done!" he explained.

"That's where I come in. What you don't know or understand is that while you live, your consciousness grows with you. By the time you are old, your consciousness has grown as big as it can in a single lifetime. Consciousness is power! When someone dies, all that consciousness is drained off back into the collective to be recycled into a new life form. For centuries, I have been content to take that consciousness from a person, one person at a time. Over the years I have grown more and more powerful, and now, there is a way for me to harvest the consciousness of millions and billions of individual humans at once. It might be better to use the term "soul" although I prefer the cleaner term of consciousness. I can collect that power and wield it here and in other parts of the universe," Walter said.

Some people call me evil. Others think I'm the devil. I prefer to think of myself as a simple galactic businessman. You see, not all creatures of the universe were granted free moral choice, but you were. There is a world of difference between mere consciousness and free moral choice. The consciousness quality and strength of a being with free moral choice is infinitely greater than any other living thing and I, I will control that power as it grows," Walter said.

"Your daughter is the gateway to the other world, to another dimension of which you are unaware. Her talents will be harnessed to serve me. She will deliver all humanity and their collective consciousness to me to process and to use at my discretion," Walter said. Then he stopped talking. He had given me all the information he thought I wanted to hear. He had grown tired of tormenting Bob and I. His words confirmed the fears my mind had conjured up over the years with the aliens. I felt the weight of the existential moment of being where I had no feeling at all and certainly no sense of any power in this situation and yet, I knew I had to do something. Somehow I knew I still had a choice. I still had a part to play in this drama and I would do whatever I needed to do to save my little girl. I just didn't know what I was going to do.

Walter was done with us. He turned his back to us and told the guards:

"Take them to the chamber. We'll' kill them and process their consciousness now." They walked out of the room. Bob and I looked at each other, only now realizing that our end had come. We never could have imagined the impact of Walter's words or his intentions or his mere presence of being. We were both powerless to resist or to do anything that our captors didn't want us to do. They wheeled us down the hall to the room as Walter had instructed. The guards rolled us both into a dark room and left. Then we waited. Bob and I lay on the operating tables staring into the inky blackness. I'm not sure how long we waited. It was impossible to tell time in the dark. Maybe it was an hour or two later when the lights came on. Walter and Jim walked into the room. Walter was beaming and said:

"Let's get this over with. I have other things to attend to this evening," And then he and Jim sat down at one end of the chamber.

The guards started moving around when the lights dimmed, then flickered, and then went completely dark. I could hear voices in the dark, people scrambling around, metal clanking metal, and then slowly, the lights came up dimly. Bob and I were struck with utter terror at what we saw! The ceiling and walls had fallen away completely. We were no longer inside a chamber. We were somewhere on a great plain. Bob and I both could see Walter and Jim sitting on the couch at the end of what was once the chamber. Jim was shocked at what was happening as well, but Walter merely stood up and began to transform into something else. As we watched, Walter changed from an elderly man to a massive and young creature standing before us. It's difficult to describe his being as he morphed into an entirely different creature right before our eyes!

His legs had grown very long and strong. He had legs like a water buffalo or huge goat, and the body of a man, but his head was like the head of an eagle, but it wasn't an eagle. It was mythological looking, like a phoenix or griffin. He had huge powerful wings and arms as well. Walter was now a very large hybrid being and from somewhere Walter was given a gigantic sword in one hand and a hatchet in the other hand. He launched himself forward and upward and was flying above the ground.

There were sounds coming from his mouth, but they were no longer human. The sound was huge and loud and shrill at the same time. His cries terrified my flesh and made me physically sick. I was no longer aware of Bob and Jim. I was lost in the terror of Levant right in front of me. He flew up and off after something or someone.

All around us his guards also began to change form. Although much smaller than Walter, they changed into creatures I find difficult to describe. They were evil. They were all pure evil beings. They seemed to change in unison and then to fly up alongside Walter. I suddenly realized there were thousands and thousands of them, all flying together! The sky was filled with them! I looked out across the great plain and it was blanketed with men turning into these creatures and taking to the air, following Walter. He was perhaps a mile or two away and still I could hear his gurgling and growling and the screeching noises coming from him. Distance did not dim his physical presence and space seemed no longer to contain him.

Bob and I were paralyzed with fear. We no longer cared we were bound or upon table. The physical reality surrounding us had engulfed us in a vortex of evil. Our minds were complete blanks except for the present moment of horror. We were captivated spellbound in this horrific demonstration of strength and terror. Our hopes sank as we knew we had come to the end of our days. We had failed. We realized our smallness in all things and our complete meaninglessness in the universe. We were both weeping, but it didn't seem to matter. Nothing seemed to matter now. All was lost. The darkness that surrounded us crept inside us and made us weak with fear.

Even at a great distance, Walter's presence held all creatures spellbound. Every living thing was focused on his being, which was presently rising in the sky and drawing all the other foul creatures to him. Just at this moment I felt something tugging at my shackles. I looked down and there was Ruth. There was my little Ruthie here with me at the final moments. In that moment I could feel my heart break completely. I had never expected to feel another human emotion after what I had just seen, but there was my baby!

"Daddy. You have to take these off. You have to get free," Ruth said with pleading eyes. Just then, Jim appeared out of nowhere and opened my shackles and gave me the keys.

"Get Bob and get out of here!" he yelled. Jim looked me right in the eyes with a wild crazed look and said: "I've got something I have to do. I hope I'm not too late!"

I watched him turn and disappear into the darkness. I was free! I was free! I grabbed Ruth and hugged her like I never hugged her before.

"Thank you honey! You've saved me!" I said looking into her eyes. She was calm, mildly calm. She was so trusting.

I jumped from the table and unchained Bob. "Come on. We've got to get out of here," I yelled as the three of us made our way across the plain to a shallow ravine. It was only three or four feet deep, but it was the only shelter we available to us. We crouched down together and I held Ruth close to me as the darkness continued to spread everywhere. If this was going to be the end of us at least Ruth was with me. I could walk through the gates of hell right now as long as I had my little girl with me. My mind was filled with only one desire, one goal: to get my

239

daughter out of here to some safe place. I just needed to rest here for a minute, to get my bearings. I needed a little time to figure out our next move.

"ANGEL OF VENGANCE"

Chapter 19

We huddled together in the ravine for what seemed like eternity. Bob and I both realized there was no more hope. Neither of us had any idea of what was going on. We were only aware of the growing darkness all around us. Ruth clung to me like a little girl hangs onto her dad when she isn't sure what's happening. Presently things began to change. We heard clearly, very clearly, the sound of trumpets! Trumpets? There was no time after that. It stopped completely and we were caught in between worlds where almost nothing at all exists.

In an instant the light came. It was the most brilliant light I had ever seen. It was brighter than looking at the sun. This light flowed right through us. There were white hot laser beams that flooded the darkness like a million lighthouse beacons. The lights seemed to be alive. They shimmered and moved like a million strobe lights. I had never seen such light before. Then we saw thousands and maybe millions of other creatures flying down toward Walter and his minions. There was clashing of metal. It was a deafening roar of steel on steel everywhere at once. There was screaming and yelling and we knew the end of the world had come upon us. The level of violence and struggle consumed all of us. We could smell the violence in the air we were breathing and taste it on our lips. We were in the middle of a violent storm and a struggle for life. It was the battle of good versus evil, playing out right in front of us. We didn't know anything anymore. We were simply there in that place, together.

This fighting raged on for hours and hours and hours. It might as well have been all eternity for us. There was no time anymore, only the terror of an unending moment of agony. As the battle raged on we could see everyone drifting slowly back to earth. The storm began to settle like a fog on the ground, back to the plain where we were hiding. After an exhausting eternity, we could see everyone on the ground now. There were still hundreds of soldiers all fighting with swords clashing at each other, and slaying thousands on both sides.

We knew we couldn't stay where we were forever, so at one point we decide to make a run for it. We didn't get very far before we were pinned down. Bob and I grabbed swords from the fallen and began fighting hand to hand as best we could. And then we saw him! There was Gabe, a brilliant light in a sea of darkness. He was massive! He was way bigger than I had ever seen him and he had huge wings, like Walter's. He was fighting Walter! They were hacking and slashing at each other with neither one giving ground. All I could think of was somehow getting Ruth out of here, out of the way, to some place safe. We kept retreating away from the battle, slowly, very slowly.

Then suddenly, I couldn't retreat any further. There was an unknown force that possessed me and held me in place. It overpowered my sense of self-preservation and everything I valued. I was thunderstruck that even my love for Ruth, my instinct to protect her, all drained away and yielded to this strength I felt rising inside me. It was a force I had not felt before, nor could I explain it, but I would not leave. I grabbed Ruth in one arm and in my other arm I had a sword. I turned toward Gabe and Walter and then started walking toward them.

"Doug! What are you doing?" Bob screamed into my ear. "Doug! Doug!" I heard him yelling. I was focused on Walter now and nothing was going to stop me!

As we approached Gabe and Walter, it became apparent how evenly matched they were. Neither one was going to defeat the other, yet they fought on. When we finally got close enough I yelled:

"Stop! Stop this fighting now!" and they all stopped! Everything became quiet and still. Gabe and Walter stopped fighting and both turned their gaze toward us.

"Walter looked at me and smiled.

"Well, come to see how this all ends?" he smirked.

"No Walter. I came to see the end of you!" I said. Gabe was watching the events unfold in front of him, but was at the ready to block any move Walter might make.

"It's over Walter. You're done here. You cannot have my daughter! I will not let her go." I said defiantly.

"You don't have a choice Doug." Walter said with a quiet smile that unnerved me. He lunged toward me with his sword coming down on us. I saw Walter's face, frozen in time, in front of me staring right through my flesh with burning red eyes. His expression revealed an eternity of anguish and a deep sense of hopelessness and cruelty.

The next thing that happened is beyond belief. It's really beyond description. I could see Walter's sword swinging down on me and I was lifting mine to deflect his blow when his sword stopped! It never reached my sword. I clearly saw Walter's face, twisted and contorted with pain...and something else....surprise. Walter was surprised as he looked to his right and there was Jim, standing next to me with a long spear. He must have come up from behind us and just at the moment that Walter began to strike, Jim had thrust a spear into his side!

At the same moment, Gabe had closed the ground between them and lobbed off Walter's head with a single swing of his sword. Instantly Walter's entire physical body disintegrated into a million sparkling lights and floated to the ground. He was gone. It was over. The battle was over. The entire world fell silent and Walter's minions slid off into the darkness. I didn't know what to think. I grabbed Ruth and hugged her close. She was terrified and yet very calm. My daughter had a strange knowing look on her face. As I focused my attention on her I saw for the first time that she was holding a sword in her hand! I wanted to cry, but had no tears left. I was numb!

"We gotta get home to mommy. She's going to be mad because we've been gone so long," Ruth said.

"We'll worry about mommy soon enough little princess," I said and gave her a big kiss.

Bob was sitting close and we just looked at each other in disbelief. Neither of us could fathom the events we had just witnessed. We were both in a state of shock. All we could manage was to simply lie there together and feel the calm and the warmth of the desert wrapping us all up into a single embrace. In an instant Jim was there by our sides. How he found us, I don't know.

"You guys made it! I'm so relieved! Sorry Doug. I was on a special assignment. So glad you didn't blow my cover with Walter. I hope you have no hard feelings. Just for the record, I was never far from Gabe and company. They sent me to Walter. They sent me to infiltrate his organization after I had recruited you. That's why I disappeared. It wasn't an assignment I wanted, but I'm always one to follow orders. These guys really do know what they're doing," he said with a sheepish smile.

My heart felt better hearing Jim's words. This whole thing was traumatic. It's not the thing a normal person ever has to endure. It's an extraordinary thing and I was exhausted. My only comfort in this mess was holding my little girl and knowing she was safe, knowing I would make her safe, and also, somehow knowing she was way more than what she appeared to be. She was my incredible daughter who I was so proud of on this day. She actually was the one that set the stage for Walter's fall. This was one of those surreal moments out of time. There was no time in this place anymore. We no longer inhabited bodies. We were simply there as a presence, as individual witnesses to what had just occurred and we rest in those moments.

Oddly, the next few minutes were the calmest moments of my life. I was totally at peace with myself as if I had become one with the universe. In those few moments I understood completely the meaning of life. I didn't need to read any scrolls or take any more lessons. Holding my daughter and feeling the warm sand underneath me, I knew the depth and breadth of life as a man, as a human being. We are only in this place for a finite time. How we choose to use it will decide the fate of everything. Although we perceive ourselves as only a small part of humanity, the choices we make, every choice we make, has consequences. Some of them are very small and others create ripples across the ocean of time that sends a gigantic waves crashing into an unknown shore somewhere. We are all responsible for what we think and for the choices we make.

Presently I was aware of a great light and looking up I saw Gabe standing above me. He was huge! He was bigger and brighter than I had ever seen him. This must be his true form I thought as I looked up at him. His kindly face looked down on me and Bob and my little girl and he said,

"You've done well this day my son, but it was not your strength alone that save you. Your daughter has a pure faith in good. And your love for her together with that faith turned the tide of evil this day. If that were not true, my sword could not do the work in was forged to do this day," Gabe said solemnly. "I give thanks for our victory knowing it is only a temporary one, but a victory none the less."

After a while we collected ourselves and got up. We walked around a bit and then Gabe and Micah came back and said,

"You must come with us now." And so we followed them into a room that had appeared near where we were standing. In an instant we were all flying above the earth, traveling to some unknown destination. I had done this so much that I wasn't worried anymore. I had no idea where we were going, but we were with Gabe and Micah, so it would be okay.

Presently Gabe opened the door and we all walked out into the main dining area of Emma's. I knew this place well. Jim and I just looked at each other and smiled. Bob was confused as hell and seriously had no idea what was happening to him. We all sat at a table together and the waiter cook brought us all something to drink. It looked like we were all going to have lunch together at Emma's. I looked at Bob and said, "Well, finally, you and I are going to actually have an uneventful lunch together. Welcome to Emma's Chuck Wagon!"

"THE BENEFACTOR OF SOULS"

Chapter 20-Epilogue

Things didn't end there that day at Emma's. For Jim, it was the completion of a particularly difficult assignment, one that he would prefer to not be asked to repeat under any circumstances. For Bob, it was his introduction to the real software that was running the planet. He was pleased and elated and fully appreciated every nuance and aspect of his new found association. Bob was going to be a player in this game going forward. No longer would he be simply the bait.

We sat and talked and listened to each other's stories for maybe hours. I kept recalling bits and pieces of conversations from over the years and something else… disconnected images that never seemed to make sense or mean anything. Some of those pieces began coming together and then I remembered the spear!

"Jim, how did you know that spear would stop Walter?" I asked as the question seemed to pop into my head.

"It took me several years to get close to Walter Harrison. He was very thorough, never trusting anyone. Over time, he came to enjoy my company in some way. I think he felt he needed a witness and that I was a good audience for his evil deeds. Maybe he felt it was important for him to have someone share his evil insanity. After many years, Walter invited me to his home. I was shocked and also touched that he trusted me enough to invite me into his private life. But Walter had an ulterior motive for my visit," Jim explained

"Walter had a special room, a secret room, where he kept his most valuable possessions. He showed me this room. It was filled with ancient and esoteric relics from all ages and places.

249

The collect was extraordinary! It was beyond imagination. He had a sword he claimed had belonged to Genghis Khan. There was a knife and shield he said belonged to Alexander the Great. There was a pair of ivory tusks from a wooly mammoth and a stuffed head of a saber tooth tiger. He showed me fragments of stone and claimed they were all that remained of the original Ten Commandments," he said with a sense of awe as he remembered the relics he had seen once.

"There was a bowl, a gold bowl filled with the broken remnants from the rings of the popes! He showed me his prize possession. He told me that above all other things; he loved this thing the most. It was the spear you saw me holding when I stabbed Walter," Jim said with a pause.

"Why was that so special? What was so special about that spear?" I asked.

"That spear holds a great power. It was the Lance of Longinus! It's known to the world as The Lance of Destiny!" Jim explained.

"What does that mean? I never heard of it," I said not understanding.

"Longinus was a Roman centurion and was the soldier assigned to insure that Jesus of Nazareth was dead. It was his spear that pierced the side of Christ on the cross!" Jim said with a sobering tone in his voice. I looked around the room and saw the expression on Gabe's face as he listened to Jim explain. It was the saddest face I had ever seen. I didn't know what it meant and couldn't bring myself to ask. Everyone sat there in silence for a while, contemplating everything that happened.

"Jim, why did you drug us? Bob and I were planning on storming the place. Why did you drug us?" I asked.

"It was the only way to keep you safe. Had you tried to break into the compound, Walter's guards would have killed you. I knew if I could deliver you both, there would be a chance to work out a rescue for all three of you...actually for all four of us. I still held Walter's confidence at that point." Jim explained.

For me and Ruth it was a different story altogether. I had been part of this program for so many years and had done my best to deny its existence. Yet, here we all were, playing our parts and being part of the continuation of the process that holds the fabric of the universe together. All we ever are, very simply, is who we are at any given moment in time. I was especially proud of Ruth. She is so young and hasn't had time to form a mature personality, so what we saw from her came from her heart. It is the stuff of who she is! How could a father be more proud of a daughter than I am of my little girl? She saved my life today!

Gabe sat down at our table and for an instant I flashed through a decade of memories of him. He was always such an imposing figure, but nothing like what I saw today.

"Gabe, what does this all mean? What happened out there on that plain today? Can you explain it to me? Can you give me some words of wisdom I can take home into this world we live in and make sense out of all that I witnessed today?" I asked with a pure heart.

"Doug, we've known each other now for many years. Some of what happened today I was able to see coming. I am not God. I cannot see the future, but I can help to prepare myself and others for what I can see coming our way. We have no choice

251

but to live in time now. We live "in time." That is a key ingredient to the work we do. It is a dimension we must consider when we act. There have been many actions between us that have happened "out of time" because we can manage time, but we cannot overcome it," he said.

"What saved you today? What saved all of us really is this: Ruth had the faith in her dad and the love for her dad to act! She did not hesitate to wield the sword of her heart and soul to fend off the evil. Her heart did not waiver! That is a pure act Doug! Even Levant's power cannot stand against such power. Ruth, with her limited human strength and her free will, was able to summon strength and power from the universe that honored the lance that Jim used to stop Levant. Her single purpose and intent was to protect you, and everything she loved in a single moment. In that moment, Levant was defeated. This is how we have kept peace in the universe as long as I can remember. There have already been so many battles that have been fought." Gabe said looking right through me with a steely gaze.

"Despite all the crazy ideas that get put forth by your people, there is only one force that remains eternal, and that is love. Love can never be destroyed and once felt, once embraced, it will go on forever. That is how it has always been. I and the beings that serve with me have been commissioned by a power greater than us to be protectors of the people of earth. For in this place, humans have received the gift of free will, which is a prize that is rare even throughout the entire universe. You must guard it with your heart. Only love can protect it and make it yield the great power it contains." Gabe said.

He told me many other things that were of great interest. We talked and talked for what seemed like days while we were at

Emma's. He told me that they would be contacting me again at some point, that they needed me to continue to work with them to make the world a better place. Most importantly, he told me that Ruth had very special powers that would need my strength and wisdom to bring to fruition as she grew into a woman. He charged me with her guardianship and her custody for a time.

"All things happen in their time as each man has his season. Ruth has not yet begun her own journey. You must do what you can to teach her the things she will need and give her the skills she will need for her time." Gabe said.

We sat there together for a while longer. Ruth had gone to sleep in my lap. I pondered Gabe's words and advice and realized that it's never really over, that life goes on and on, and each of us simply plays our part when it's our time. Looking at Gabe I also realized that Ruth was somehow going to have a big part in the future of the planet in her role working with the Caretakers. I was now not only her dad, but a kind of life coach. Ruth would get the best training a father could provide. There was no doubt in my mind that Ruth would lead a very interesting life.

I called Mary and told her I was bringing our little girl home to her family and hopefully to a better life.

The End

The second book in this series is called "Hyperion Rising." Please join us as the adventure continues with the next generation.

www.ingramcontent.com/pod-product-compliance
Lightning Source LLC
Chambersburg PA
CBHW072226190626
46809CB00017B/746